CROSSROADS
VOLUME 1

N.L. MCLAUGHLIN

TWISTED SKY

Copyright © 2024 by N.L. McLaughlin

All rights reserved.

No part of this book may be reproduced in any form or by any electronic or mechanical means, including information storage and retrieval systems, without written permission from the author, except for the use of brief quotations in a book review.

To Robert
My best friend, partner in crime and the love of my life.

"I am the spirit that negates.
>   And rightly so, for all that comes to be
>   Deserves to perish wretchedly"

> - JOHANN WOLFGANG VON GOETHE, FAUST,
> PART ONE

TEN

CROSSROADS
VOLUME 1

CHAPTER 1

THE MIDNIGHT SKY was black as pitch, not a single star in sight. Even the moon was nowhere to be seen, hidden by the dense clouds that hung in the sky like a suffocating shroud.

"I do so hate it when it's like this," said Nine. "It makes this place feel more like a prison than usual."

Les glanced over at the apparition slithering close like a sleek, iridescent serpent. "My dear, are you saying that you feel trapped here?" He gestured with his hands. "Why this place is paradise. Isn't that what we were told it would be?"

He leaned down and lit a cigarette. Exhaling a plume of smoke, he said, "Who could have guessed that humans would take something so precious as the Garden of Eden and turn it into a slum." He gazed up at the sky.

"My dear Mephistopheles, you're waxing philosophical tonight," said Nine. "Have the years taken their toll on you? Are you getting soft?"

"Now, Nine, you know I go by Les these days," he said. "The young folks don't like complicated names." He exhaled a cloud of smoke. "And to answer your question, no.

I'm not getting soft. If anything, the longer I'm here and the more contact I must maintain with these loathsome meat puppets, the more I despise them." He raked his fingers through his dark, shiny hair. "Everything was given to them. Much more than any of us. And what have they done with it? They tear down mountains, contaminating the soil and turning the water to filth, all in the name of saving the planet. Endless wars, famine, plague; the extent of destruction they have brought is far beyond anything we could have ever dreamed. Even their bodies are filled to the brim with envy, lust, greed and all the other seven deadly sins. You name it, they're wallowing in it."

"You should try living inside one," said Nine as she swirled around his head. "Their minds are terribly dark places." She chuckled softly. "I must admit, I find it rather enjoyable."

"I'm good on the possession thing," he replied. "I rather like my body. I find myself quite attractive." He grinned.

"Of course you do," replied Nine. "Narcissus would have nothing on you, my old friend."

He took one last drag from the cigarette, then tossed it on the ground and stamped it out with the toe of his boot. Making a performance of waving Nine's misty form away from him, Les said, "When I agreed to this venture, I never imagined you would be a part of it." He stopped waving his arms. "What did he offer you to be involved?"

"The usual," said Nine. "An all-encompassing thrill ride into chaos and destruction." She swirled overhead. "What made you agree to this adventure?"

"I wouldn't miss it for the world," he replied. "I've had the luxury of being around every time our friend has made an appearance." His lips curled into a malevolent grin. "I just love the chaos he creates. The fear, anarchy and pure savagery of it all is a sight to behold. He's a genuine artist. It's a wonderful time for all. Except, of course, for the victims."

"He's playing a long game this time," said Nine.

Les nodded in agreement. "That he is. He's one of the most patient demons I've ever known. His current plan demonstrates that perfectly."

"What if the humans decide to change course somehow?" she asked. "What if they refuse to go along?"

"I'm sure he's taken that into consideration. Our dear old friend most assuredly has a backup plan. He's itching to be a part of the human world again. One way or another, he will be back, and he will wreak havoc in that special way that only he can."

"Your voice is full of adoration."

"I have the deepest respect for him—for what he does."

The sound of a vehicle approaching cut through the night. Les gazed out along the deserted highway just in time to see a pair of headlights rushing toward them.

"Well," he said with a sigh. "Looks like it's time. Tonight, we kick off a chain of events that will, in due time, shatter the pathetic lives of countless many."

"I will leave you to your task then," said Nine. "I'll see you when it's my turn to take part." Without another word, she gathered herself and floated through the air, just another small cloud in the evening sky. In a flash of iridescent mist, she disappeared.

The vehicle raced forward, its tires screeching against the asphalt, hurtling towards the crossroad. He extended his mind, feeling the rush of wind against his skin as he delved into the driver's consciousness. Amidst the chaos of her thoughts, he sensed a palpable mix of heartache, resignation, seething anger, and a desperate yearning for an end.

But not tonight, he silently resolved. Tonight, amidst her vulnerability, he would present her with an extraordinary opportunity to obtain everything she ever dreamed of.

With a casual wave of his hand, Les effortlessly guided the vehicle off the paved road, its tires crunching on the gravel as it smoothly transitioned onto the grassy terrain, coming to an abrupt stop.

He cleared his throat, then straightened his clothes, feeling the crisp fabric against his skin. He inhaled; his entire body tingled with the promise of chaos. He could hardly wait to see the pieces of this malevolent puzzle fall into place. The thrill surged through his veins, electrifying his every nerve. He so enjoyed ruining the lives of these silly humans, reveling in their misery. With a final sigh, his breath mingling with the cool evening breeze, he sauntered over to the vehicle.

CHAPTER 2
NINETEEN YEARS LATER

THE VAST DESERT stretched out before Riley as the car raced along at seventy miles an hour. She couldn't resist the temptation and rolled down her window, inviting a rush of warm air to caress her face. The distinct aroma of desert sage and mesquite filled her nostrils. As her gaze wandered upwards, she was captivated by the mesmerizing spectacle of the night sky adorned with a myriad of twinkling stars. A deep sense of happiness enveloped her as cherished memories of countless road trips with her family flooded her thoughts.

Beside her, Mason slept propped up against his door, mouth open, emitting soft snores that filled the air. A thin rivulet of drool escaped down his chin, leaving a faint glistening trail.

Fraternal twins—that's what they were. Born twenty minutes apart, Riley, being the oldest, never missed an opportunity to remind him that he was her baby brother. Mason would always respond to her taunts with a roll of his eyes or a simple moan.

As much as she resembled their mom, her brother had

the same uncanny resemblance to their dad. From his tall stature to his head full of unruly dark brown hair, Mason could have been a carbon copy of their father. But the similarity was purely physical. Unlike their dad, Mason was an artist. Rather than play football, he chose instead to play a vast array of musical instruments and write beautiful poetry. There wasn't an instrument he couldn't master—it was almost as though he was born to be a great musician.

While she could respect his love of art, Riley simply didn't share his talent in that area. Suffice to say, she ended up being the athletic twin, and he was the moody artist.

These two differences had set them down two distinct roads. In another month, she would head off to college in Austin, where she earned herself a place on the basketball team. Mason, on the other hand, was destined for Denton where he would major in music theory and study under a faculty that was made up of premier jazz musicians.

As she watched him sleep, she couldn't deny the twinge of sadness that crept in; she would miss seeing him every day. Inwardly, she wondered if he would feel the same about her.

In the front seat, riding shotgun, her mom slept. Her long, brown hair billowing in the breeze created by Riley's open window. As a lock swirled around the headrest, Riley recalled the many times when she, as a child, would snuggle up in her momma's arms and twist a lock of hair around her tiny fingers. As memories flooded back, she remembered how, as a young child, she would beam with pride whenever others drew comparisons between her and her mother. In her eyes, Haley was the most beautiful woman in the world.

Fighting back tears, Riley closed her eyes, telling herself to stop, she was being ridiculous. She was going away to college; her family wasn't dying. As her mom would always say, they were simply moving into a new phase in their lives. Every ending brings a new beginning.

"You look as though you're a million miles away," said her dad, as he peered at her through the rear-view mirror. His lips were curled into that familiar, warm smile of his.

Riley smiled back. "Just thinking of all the trips we took growing up."

He nodded and turned his gaze to the open road. "So, am I to assume you're glad we made this a road trip instead of flying?"

"Okay," said Riley. "Don't let it go to your head, but you were right." She glanced out the window. "How much longer do you think we have?"

"My best guess is several hours," replied Wade. "We're pretty far out. You know, you could take a page from your mom and brother and get some rest."

Riley shook her head. "And leave you alone? Pshh." She waved her hand dismissively. "Someone has to stay awake with you, so you don't fall asleep and kill us all."

"Such faith in my abilities," he replied, feigning insult. He chuckled. "But seriously, I've got this. You can rest. I might be getting older, but I can still party all night."

"Nice try old man," said Riley. "I've seen you passed out in the living room at seven o'clock."

"That one hurt," said Wade, playfully clutching his chest as though he were in pain. "I'll have you know, there was a time when I could be up for days."

"Uh, huh," said Riley, smirking. "That was what, three decades ago?"

"Decades? Young lady, exactly how old do you think I am?"

Riley shrugged. "I don't know, fifty or so?"

Her dad gasped and let his mouth drop open.

"I mean," continued Riley. "You have all that gray hair."

"Hey now, every one of these gray hairs was caused by you and your brother."

"Whatever makes you feel better," she giggled.

"Seriously," said Wade. "Your entire tween stage, all that money to straighten teeth, let's not forget the whole learning to drive fiasco. And your brother, don't even get me started. Do I need to remind you of the time he blew up the hay bales behind the barn?"

"That was not my fault," said Mason. He sat up and wiped the drool from the corner of his mouth. "Ri—"

"He's right," said Riley, as she glared at Mason to silence him. "It was all an accident."

Mason glared at her. Truth was, the great hay bale event was caused by her and her best friend, Lilly. They had been smoking weed behind the barn. Mason was busy playing with firecrackers while standing watch for them. High and not really thinking right, it was Riley who lit the firecracker, then tossed it right onto a bale, when it nearly exploded in her hand. Her brother took the blame and the punishment.

"Who's right?" asked Haley as she sat up and adjusted her seat. She glanced around the vehicle with sleepy eyes.

Wade reached out and took her hand in his. "We're just chatting about all the fun times we've had over the years."

Haley yawned and nodded her head. She peered out the window. "Where are we?"

"About four miles outside of Toyah," said Wade.

"How are you feeling? Do you need me to do some of the driving?" she asked.

"I got this," he replied. "In spite of the fact that your daughter thinks I'm old." He grinned at Riley through the rear-view mirror.

"Aw," said Haley. "You're not old." She ran her fingers through his hair. "I think the gray makes you look sexy."

"Oh, ew," said Riley in mock disgust.

Mason groaned, mimicking her reaction.

"What?" teased Haley as she turned around to grin at them. "I'll have you know; your father is a very sexy man."

"Now look what you started," said Mason.

"Seriously," continued their mom, with an impish glint in her eyes. "You two wouldn't even be here if he wasn't as sexy as he is."

Wade laughed heartily.

"That's it," said Mason, pulling his hood over his head and shrinking back into his seat. "I'm out. Goodnight." He folded his arms across his chest and rested his head against the window.

Riley wasn't about to let them win that easily. "Just keep your eyes on the road, lover boy," she said. I'd like to get home in one piece."

"No worries," replied Wade, glancing at her through the mirror. "I've got everything under control."

"Wade!" shouted Haley. "Look out!"

Riley glanced out the windshield, just in time to see the biggest coyote she had ever seen standing in the middle of the road. The beast made no attempt to move out of the way. It stood its ground and fearlessly stared into the vehicle. Its eyes glowed like ice blue fire.

Wade swerved the steering wheel and hit the brakes, but he lost control.

Riley and Haley screamed as the vehicle crashed over the guardrail and tumbled down into a ravine. As they rolled over and over, her head smashed into the window, eventually shattering it. Her ears rang as her head screamed out in pain.

CHAPTER 3

"*BE CALM,*" a haunting whisper echoed through Mason's mind, its ethereal cadence filling his thoughts.

Who are you? he thought. The words need not be spoken aloud, for the voice resonated within his mind.

His body stirred involuntarily, as if animated by an invisible force. The rhythmic jostling intensified. The faint scent of gasoline wafted on the air as his senses gradually returned.

"Mase! Mase!" shouted his father. The sound of his voice echoed faintly, as if coming from far away, yet close at the same time.

With a sudden, jarring force, a sharp slap landed across his face, sending waves of pain radiating through his cheek. Startled, he fought against the heaviness weighing down his eyelids, straining to pry them open.

"Look at me!" shouted Wade.

Mason groaned, his eyelids heavy and resistant. Gradually, his eyes fluttered open, revealing the blurry figure of his father looming above him. He blinked, trying to focus, but the world spun around him relentlessly. Nausea overwhelmed him. With his hand desperately pressed against his mouth, Mason leaned over and violently expelled the contents of his stomach.

As the world ceased its dizzying dance, his eyes settled upon the worried face of his mother.

"What happened?" he asked, suddenly realizing he was not in the vehicle, but sitting on the rocky ground.

"Stay put," said his mother as she pressed a gentle hand against his chest. "Your father's getting Riley." She wiped a soft cloth across his face. "You weren't wearing your seat belt, so you got tossed around. You're lucky you didn't break your neck."

That explained the throbbing pain he felt in the side of his head. It also explained the nausea. He reached up and touched the spot where the pain emanated, pulling his hand away, he stared at his fingers coated in warm, fresh blood.

"Haley, come on over and help me," shouted his father.

His mother gave a quick nod, then turned back to Mason. "You stay here. I'll be right back." Then she was gone.

He sat alone, listening to the sound of his parent's panicked voices as they tried to awaken Riley. The smell of burnt rubber mixed with oil and gasoline. Intermittent plumes of smoke billowed in the soft evening breeze, creating a surreal, almost ghostly setting.

Somewhere out in the hills that surrounded them, a lone coyote called, followed by a cacophony of what could only be described as laughter from an unseen pack.

The faint sound of leaves rustling softly in the dense brush nearby caught his attention. Mason turned his head in that direction, kicking off another wave of nausea. As he strained his eyes, the spindly limbs of a desert plant obstructed his view, forcing him to squint and peer through the tangled foliage. A sudden movement startled him, too fleeting for his mind to comprehend. A surge of fear welled up in his gut. He rubbed his eyes, trying to clear his vision, and leaned in closer.

Two black eyes stared back at him through the dark.

A soft sound, reminiscent of a child's gleeful giggle, danced through the air.

Confused, Mason remained motionless, his eyes straining to process what his mind refused to understand.

"He's pretty," whispered a child's voice, followed by more giggles and excited whispers.

More eyes appeared in the shadows. They studied him, never blinking—emotionless.

A profound, chilling sense of foreboding washed over him. The desert breeze now turned icy, devoid of any life.

In the depths of darkness, the haunting eyes flickered, emitting a faint glow before vanishing.

He moved his head from side to side and blinked, there was no sign of the otherworldly eyes. Had he imagined them? Was his head injury making him hallucinate? His mind told him this had to be the case, but his instinct told him to be afraid—very afraid. As his confusion swirled, the pain in his head subsided.

"Fear not," said the strange man's voice from earlier. *"All will be as it should be."*

"Dad?" said Mason, his voice sounding small in his own ears.

No one answered.

He turned toward the vehicle where he saw both his mother and father, leaning inside, speaking rapidly to one another, no doubt working to free Riley from the wreckage. So, whose voice just whispered to him?

Every muscle in his body trembled with fear. Mason

moved his gaze along the perimeter that was visible to his naked eyes. As far as he could see, there was nothing out there.

First a giggling child, and now some invisible man, he must have really hit his head hard. For the first time since coming to, Mason wondered if he had suffered some sort of brain damage from the accident. He stared down at his hands, moving each finger, then his wrists and finally his arms. At least nothing was broken.

Sitting on the hard, rocky ground, he took stock of the rest of his body. From what he could tell, he suffered no serious injuries. His head still throbbed, but a gentle touch with his fingers told him the bleeding had stopped. It appeared as though the only injury he suffered was a rather large welt on the side of his head.

And of course, hearing the voices.

The sound of what could only be described as something scraping along in the dirt startled him. Mason snapped his head in the direction, only to end up regretting that move. He moaned and raised his hand to his temple, willing the world to stop swirling. He stared at the cluster of desert plants close by; positive that, at any moment, a child or some strange man would pop out.

The shifting grew louder.

Mason's gut told him to get up and run, but his body refused to cooperate.

The spindly limbs of the brush shook and trembled as the sound grew louder. He thought about calling for his parents, but his throat was too dry and constricted.

The brush shook, then suddenly an armadillo waddled out into the open. The creature stopped and stared at Mason, just as shocked to see him as he was, then it turned and ran back into the brush.

Mason sighed in relief. With a halfhearted chuckle, he scolded himself for letting his imagination get the best of him. There was nothing out here but small desert creatures and his family.

The subtle sound of a child's giggle floated on the air.

CHAPTER 4

THE DISTANT ECHOES of her mother and father's urgent voices reached her ears, mingling with the sound of her own heartbeat pounding in her chest. With a trembling hand, she reached up, fingertips brushing against the sticky warmth on the side of her head, feeling tiny granules of glass. The metallic scent of blood invaded her nostrils, causing her stomach to churn.

"Riley! Riley! Answer me baby!" cried her mother.

A heaviness settled in her head, while her lower body felt almost weightless.

Something was pressing against her waist, holding her down—or up. *Am I hanging upside down?* Her long hair dangled below her, answering her own question.

Images like an old movie flashed in her mind.

The coyote. Mason crashing, headfirst, toward the roof of the vehicle. Her mind grappled with the meaning of that, then she realized that he fell because they were tumbling.

"Riley! Do you hear me baby?" begged her mom. The tone in her mother's voice made her afraid. She had never heard her sound so terrified before.

"I—I'm okay," she managed to mutter in reply.

Her father was beside her, upside down. She wanted to giggle at the absurdity of her current situation, but her head hurt too much.

"Okay, sweetheart," said her dad in a calm tone. She could feel his muscular arms around her. "I'm gonna release your seatbelt. Don't worry, I got you. If you can help, I'm gonna need you to do what you can."

Not able to do much, Riley nodded.

An audible click echoed through the air, followed by an abrupt onslaught of gravity. It yanked her body downwards, plunging her headfirst. Acting on instinct, she extended her arms, trying to shield her head from the impact. Feeling her father's arms holding her aloft. She relinquished control and let him gently slide her out of the vehicle.

A moment later, she was carried over and placed gently on the rocky ground beside Mason.

Nausea clawed at her insides, its grip tightening with every passing second. Unable to fight it any longer, she hunched over, her body convulsing as she emptied her stomach, the acrid scent of bile filling the air. Relief washed over her, the nausea finally subsiding, leaving in its wake the relentless throb in her head.

"Here," said her mom. "Drink some of this." She shoved a bottle of water in Riley's hand.

"What happened?" she asked as she took hold of the bottle and unscrewed the cap.

"A giant animal ran out into the road," explained her father. "I had to swerve to avoid hitting it." He glanced back at the upside-down vehicle. "I guess I over corrected."

"It's okay," said her mom. "We're all okay, so it'll be fine."

"What the hell was that?" asked Mason, his words were

slurred as though he too were regaining the proper use of his brain. He pointed to a patch of shrubs nearby. "Did you see that?" His face was a mask of fear.

"It's okay sweetheart," said Haley, handing him a bottle of water. "Take a drink." She swept an errant lock of hair away from his eyes. "There's nothing out there. You hit your head pretty hard. Try to relax. Everything's okay."

With trembling hands, he took a sip of water and rubbed his head, never truly looking away from the brush.

Riley had never seen him like this before. Fear welled up inside her as she followed his gaze.

Nothing—she saw nothing. Maybe their mom was right—there was nothing out there.

The sound of coyote chatter echoed off the hills.

Wade climbed to his feet and crept over to the vehicle where he pulled the handgun from the glove box. Weapon held up in front of him, he tiptoed around the vehicle toward the road. A moment later, he returned, stuffing the gun in his belt behind his back.

"Your mom's right," he said with a sigh. "Nothing's out there. The coyotes are far away from us." Wade raked his fingers through his hair and scanned the area as though he were trying to be sure.

The look of concern on his face wasn't a usual occurrence. Riley had all she could do to control her emotions. If her dad was worried, things must be bad.

"Phone's useless," said Haley.

Riley pulled out her phone and stared down at the screen. Nothing. There was no signal. Panic churned in her belly as she peered up at her father for reassurance.

"Makes sense," Wade said with a sigh. "We're in the middle of nowhere."

"So, what do we do now?" asked Haley.

Riley gazed back and forth at her parents as they spoke, hoping they had a plan or some way out of this mess they presently found themselves in.

"There's probably service a little way up the road," said Wade. "Or at least an emergency call box. I'll take a walk until I find something, then call for help." He gazed out along the deserted highway.

"I'll come along," said Riley.

"You can hardly sit upright," said her mom.

Riley shook her head. The last thing she wanted to do was sit there and wait. "I'm feeling okay, she blurted. "Besides, I might feel better if I walk a little. Dad shouldn't go alone."

"Then I'll go with him," said Haley.

Mason tried to stand only to have Haley gently push him back. "I'll go with him."

"No," said Wade. "You and your mom stay here with the vehicle. Maybe a semi or State Trooper will roll by. If they do, we'll need you to flag them down. I can go alone."

Determined to go along, Riley rose to her feet. "I'm coming too." Her father opened his mouth to say something, but she held up her hand to quiet him. "You're not talking me out of this. You're not going alone. Mom can take better care of Mason than I can. I'm better off helping you."

"What if those things are still out there?" asked Mason, his voice heavy with fear as he scanned the darkness that surrounded them.

"Sweetheart," said Haley. "There's nothing out there."

Wade pulled the handgun from his belt and handed it over to Haley. "If you see any sign of an animal, you shoot."

"What are you gonna use for protection?" asked Haley as she reached for the weapon.

"We'll be fine," said Wade. He locked eyes with Riley. "Are you sure you're up for this?"

Riley did a silent assessment of her situation. Headache aside, the rest of her was perfectly fine. She nodded at her father. "I'm good."

"Okay then," said Wade. "Let's see if we can get some help."

Before leaving, they loaded a backpack with some water and a few supplies, just in case. After a round of hugs, they strolled off down the highway in search of a signal, town, or some help of any kind.

CHAPTER 5

HALEY WATCHED the silhouettes of Wade and Riley disappear from view. Was this the right course of action? Were there any other choices available to them? She shook her head. Wade was right, there really was no other option. She turned and assessed the state of their vehicle, upside down laying in the ravine. There was no way whatsoever that they could salvage it.

A cool breeze floated down from the hillside, sending a shiver down her spine.

Something about this place was off. She scanned the darkness. Nothing. As far as the eye could see, there was nothing but vast wilderness. There wasn't even a streetlight or mile marker. Why on earth did Wade have to suggest they turn his cousin's wedding into a final family road trip?

Truth was, Haley didn't really want to go. As the only child of an only child, she had no extended family. But Wade, being painfully close with every relative ever born in the Davis clan, insisted it was the right thing to do. Family was always so important to him. So much so, it seemed their weekends were always taken by some function or another.

She strolled over to the vehicle and reached inside, pulling out her sweatshirt. "Do you want a blanket or something?" she asked Mason.

"I'm good," he said, never really looking over at her, instead staring off into the darkness.

As if things weren't bad enough, he was seeing things in the shadows. Haley couldn't help but wonder about the severity of his injuries.

Peering intently through squinted eyes, she swept her gaze over the brush in an effort to glimpse whatever was making him so uneasy. All the while, she silently prayed, hoping that he was indeed hallucinating. She felt awful for that, but in all honesty, the last thing she wanted was to run into whatever was creeping her son out so much.

"I don't see anything honey," she said, doing her best to sound convincing.

He ran his fingers through his hair and exhaled loudly. "You're right. There's nothing out there." He turned and stared at Haley with glassy eyes. "You think they'll be okay?"

"Dad and Riley?" she asked. "If anyone would be okay out here, it would be your dad," she said. A sense of foreboding settled deep in her bones; she couldn't shake the feeling that something was out there watching.

"It's pretty wild, ain't it?" said Mason.

"What is?"

"A place like this existing." He waved his arms around. "We think it's rural where we live, up north. But this—it's on a whole new level." He retrieved the phone from his pocket and stared down at the useless device. "I mean, what kind of place has no cell service?"

Haley chuckled. "You know, it wasn't all that long ago where there was no such thing as a cell phone."

"That was the before times, mom," he said with a grin. "Way back in the nineteen hundreds."

"It wasn't all that bad," she said. "Somehow, we managed to get along without all the electronics we have today."

Searching for something pleasant to focus on, her mind drifted into the past. "You know, I was just about your age when I moved out to that small little town to live with my grandparents. Before that, the only thing I ever knew was the city."

"I must have cried that whole first week, thinking I had moved into hell. Your great grandma insisted I'd get used to it, but I didn't believe her. Then I got the job at the grocery store." A wistful smile spread across her lips. "That was when I met your father. The first time I ever laid eyes on him I fell madly in love." She moved her head slowly from side to side. "No other boy could hold a candle to him."

She gazed lovingly at her son, so handsome and tall. It was hard to believe she created such a beautiful human being. "You look just like him."

"Yeah, yeah, so you remind me at least once a month." He smiled at her.

"Because it's true." Even in the dark, she could see Mason's face turn a pale pink hue.

A child's giggle stopped them both mid laugh.

"Did you hear that?" asked Mason.

Haley felt the tiny hairs on the back of her arms stand erect. A primal sense of deep fear surged from the depths of her belly, like an ancient instinct warning her of impending danger. Her mouth opened, but she could not utter a word.

"I told you I saw something," he said. Mason cupped his hands around his mouth. "Hello? Who's out there?"

Nothing. Not even crickets.

Once again squinting her eyes, she peered out into the darkness so intently, she began to see tiny sparks of light in the edges of her vision.

"Hello!" shouted Mason. "If you're out there, speak up!"

The subtle hint of fear in his voice mirrored her own feelings.

Mason climbed to his feet and stepped forward, only to have Haley grab him by the arm and pull him back. "No!" she hissed.

To his credit, he didn't argue with her.

For what seemed to be forever, the two of them stood in silence, staring out into the darkness. Nothing but blackness peered back.

"Maybe we imagined that," said Haley, rubbing her arms against the sudden chill that descended upon her.

"Both of us?" asked Mason.

She shrugged. "Sure. Why not?"

"How?"

"I don't know," she replied. "But it's possible."

Haley wanted so much to believe her own words, but something deep inside her soul told her that she was grasping at straws.

The sound of shuffling feet across gravel met her ears. Instinctively, she reached out for her son and pulled him along as she took a step backward. Thankfully, he moved without an argument.

Something in the air had shifted. Gone was the soft breeze, heavy with the scent of desert sage, in its place was nothing. No breeze, no sage, just an intense feeling of dread.

Haley scanned the roadside, berating herself for not insisting that she and Mason go along with Riley and Wade. How stupid to separate in such a desolate area.

Eerie silence surrounded them.

The faint sound of a giggling child wafted through the night, followed by another. Haley spun around, following the direction of the sound, but couldn't see anything.

Mason leaned down and picked up a fallen tree limb. Holding it aloft, he called out to the dark, "Alright. This ain't funny anymore. Come on out now!"

Haley waited with bated breath, terrified that whoever was behind the laughter would materialize. For some reason, she feared seeing them far more than not.

Seconds ticked by, but no one appeared.

Mason let his shoulders relax. "What should we do?" he asked.

Haley didn't know. She stared down the highway in the direction where Wade and Riley had gone, then she stared out into the dark where the voices seemed to come from. Confusion took over her senses. The breeze returned, blasting the rancid stench of rotting flesh. She wrinkled her nose and held her hand to her face.

"What the hell is that smell?" asked Mason, shoving his nose inside his hoodie.

"It smells like a dead animal."

"Why didn't we smell it before?"

Haley shook her head. "I don't know," she replied. "Do I look like I have all the answers?"

He stared at her as though she had just slapped him. Under the circumstances, she may as well have.

She gave a deep sigh. "I'm sorry. I shouldn't have snapped at you."

"It's okay mom." He placed a hand on her shoulder. "It's creepy out here. This place feels wrong."

Haley couldn't agree more. "What do you say we

venture down the road and see if we can't meet up with your dad and Riley?"

"But he said to stay here in case someone comes by."

"Look around," she said. "Have you seen any sign of anyone rolling by?" She walked over to the vehicle and pulled out one of Mason's sketch pads and a pen. "Just to be sure, we'll leave a note." She scratched out a rudimentary message, then placed the paper against the driver's side window.

"There," she said as she wiped her hands off on her thighs. "Now, grab a jacket or something and let's get going."

Without another word, Mason did as he was told. A moment later, they were strolling down the blacktop, heading, as far as she knew, in the same direction that her husband and daughter had gone just a little while ago. With any luck, they would come across them at any moment.

CHAPTER 6

THE EMPTY ROAD stretched on for miles. Riley glanced back, wondering how long it had been since she last saw their vehicle. She folded her arms around herself and said, "It's kinda creepy out here."

Doing his best to sound positive and lighthearted, Wade replied, "I don't know, I kinda like it out here." He glanced around. "There's something to be said about the rugged beauty of a place like this."

"Yeah, right," scoffed Riley. "You mean besides wondering how many cannibals are roaming the hillsides?"

He chuckled. "You guys and those horror movies of yours."

An owl screeched overhead. Riley scanned the sky, unable to discern from what direction the sound came. She wondered if there were any predators around that were large enough to attack an adult human.

As if sensing her concerns, her father said, "Don't fret over the wildlife." He tapped the bowie knife hanging from his belt. "The largest animal out here is a coyote, and they don't mess with humans."

"There's always a first time."

"Don't worry, Pixie. As long as I have breath in my lungs, you have nothing to fear from anything—animal or man."

Riley couldn't help but smile. Her dad had called her Pixie for as long as she could remember. She knew he meant every word he said. Her father would destroy heaven and earth if it would keep his family safe.

"Think mom and Mase are okay?"

Wade nodded. "Yeah, they'll be fine." His lips curled into a loving smile. "Your mom is more than capable of taking care of herself. And your brother is too." He pulled out his cell phone and held it up to check for a signal. "Besides, we shouldn't be out here too much longer. Once we call for help, we'll be on our way." He shoved the device back into his pocket.

"That's if we ever get a signal," said Riley. "How is it that a place this desolate can even exist anymore?"

"I'm sure there're lots of places like this scattered about," said Wade. "Technology just hasn't stretched out this far yet." He tapped her arm with the back of his hand and pointed at a sign. "Ya see that? Civilization is close."

The sign read, Toyah, next exit.

"Is that a town?" she asked.

"It sure is. Which means there'll be someone to help."

"I sure hope so," she said. "I think I've had my fill of the wilderness."

Wade chuckled. "Don't tell the others, but me, too." He stretched his back. "I'm ready to get home and crawl into my nice, soft bed."

They left the interstate behind and walked for what seemed at least a mile until they saw the telltale signs of a small town.

Riley's heart sank as she scanned the abandoned buildings all around. As Wade walked, he held his phone aloft, only to sigh in exasperation and stuff the device back in his pocket.

"Let's see if there's a sheriff or trooper outpost or something." He scanned the empty street. "Someone's gotta be here."

The sound of a giggling child floated on the night breeze. Not entirely sure if she heard it, Riley glanced over at her father, only to find him staring off toward the direction the sound came from. His face was a mask of concern.

"You heard it too?" she asked.

"I'm not sure what I heard."

Another giggle erupted; this time it was much closer. Riley's blood ran cold, something about all of this felt off. As they passed a run-down shop, another child giggled. The sound of scuffling feet startled her. She paused and stared into the darkness between the buildings.

A child's voice whispered, *"She's pretty."*

"Dad?" said Riley. "Did you hear that?"

"Hear what?"

"A child. I could have sworn I heard a child say something."

Wade shook his head. "I didn't hear anything." He placed one of his large hands on her shoulder. "It's just this place. And all those horror movies coming back to haunt you." He flashed a smile that didn't make it to his eyes.

It was obvious to Riley that he too was feeling nervous.

"Let's just find a phone," he said. "I'd like to get back to your brother and your mom as soon as possible."

The sound of a whimpering child floated into her ears.

Her dad stopped in his tracks. "Did you hear that?" he asked.

Riley's head bobbed in agreement as she swallowed tightly, against the lump in her throat. A wave of tension rippled through her body, causing her muscles to tremble. Her breaths were quick and shallow, echoing in her ears. Her heart pounded in her chest, its rhythm resembling that of a panicked rabbit.

Wade took her by the hand. "Come on."

"Where are we going?" she said, pulling her hand back.

"I heard a child crying over here."

"Maybe it was the wind."

Her father paused and shook his head.

The sound of a sobbing child was much louder this time. Loud enough to eliminate all doubt. It was real.

"Come on, there's a kid out here that might need help," he said.

With a knot of fear tightening in her heart, Riley trailed behind her father toward a large, decrepit building. The faded sign out front, barely clinging to its metal frame, revealed the name of the place—Toyah High School. As her eyes scanned the dilapidated structure, the sight that greeted her was one of destruction. The windows stood as shattered shards, reflecting the gloom that permeated the air. The remnants of what were once grand wooden doors now lay scattered as mere splinters on the ground, a sad testament to the ravages of time. Bricks were strewn haphazardly on the ground. The walls, once pristine and proud, were now marred by graffiti.

She cautiously leaned forward; her eyes fixed on the gaping darkness of the open entryway. A chilling breeze whispered through the air, carrying the faint scent of dampness and decay. The void before her seemed to swallow all light, leaving her with an eerie sense of unease.

The child sobbed.

"Hello?" called Wade from the doorway.

"Hello?" came the voice of a child.

Something about the child's tone didn't sit right with Riley. She wanted to turn around and run as far away from this town as possible.

Wade stepped past the threshold and lifted his phone, using it as a flashlight. "Come on out, we won't hurt you," he said.

A deep, primal sense of fear settled like an icy grip on Riley's soul. Against her better judgement, she tightly clung to her father, her heart pounding in her chest, as they cautiously ventured down the dimly lit, desolate corridor. The air felt heavy and suffocating, filled with an unsettling stillness that seemed to echo their every step.

Up ahead, they could hear a child sobbing.

"It's okay," said Wade. "You can come on out. We want to help you."

The sound of hurried footsteps erupted all around them. Startled, Riley spun around and peered into a dark room. "Hello?" she called out.

A child giggled, then whispered, *"I like her. Can she stay with us?"*

"Dad," she said. "Did you hear that?"

Wade was busy focusing on the path ahead. He didn't seem to have heard anything.

"I think the cries are coming from down here," he said.

Riley took hold of his hand and pulled back. "Can we go, please? We can go find help and bring it back."

"If there's a kid down here, we need to help them," said Wade. "I know if it were you or Mason out here, I'd want someone to help you." He strolled down the hall.

As they passed each room, the sound of shuffling feet and giggling children followed.

Deep panic welled up in Riley's chest as she forced her legs to move to keep up with her father. As much as she wanted to turn around and run away, she was far too terrified to do it alone.

The sobbing grew louder. They stopped in front of a set of heavy doors that led to the gymnasium. From where she stood, it sounded like the sobs were coming from inside.

Wade pushed open the doors with a loud, sustained creak that bounced off the walls. He moved his flashlight around in the darkness.

It's time to pay the Piper, was scrawled in giant letters across the wall in what appeared to be red paint—or blood. Following the sound, Riley and Wade crept across the gym floor and around the back of the bleachers where they found a small silhouette standing against the wall.

"It's okay," said Wade. "We're here to help." He held out his hand for the child. "Come on. We'll take you home."

Something about all of this was terribly wrong. Riley's breath came in spurts, she was sure she would pass out any moment.

The child stopped sobbing. It turned around then took a step forward, into the light.

What stood before them was no child. It appeared to be one, in size and shape. Even its face was cherubic, but the eyes—the eyes were deep, opal pools of blackness. In stark terror, Riley watched as its mouth stretched into a wide, demonic grin.

"Pretty girl. Would you like to stay with us?" said the creature in a singsong voice.

Laughter erupted all around them, shaking the bleachers, threatening to collapse on top of them. Barely aware of what was happening and unable to look away from the eyes of the child, Riley felt herself being dragged along by her hand. She glanced down to find that Wade was dragging her down the corridor and back outside.

CHAPTER 7

AS SHE SEARCHED the desolate highway, Haley was hoping to see Wade and Riley, but to no avail. They were nowhere in sight. Where the hell had they gone? Did they finally get a signal and call for help? That's stupid, Haley, she scolded herself. If they managed to do that, they would have crossed paths by now.

All around them, the shadows seemed to dance and move. She swore she could hear the eerie sound of shuffling feet.

When they came upon the road sign letting them know that Toyah was the next exit, she allowed a sigh of relief escape her lips. Finally, something positive.

Leaving the desolate highway behind, they headed toward the town. Odds were, Wade and Riley went this way. It was the only route that made sense. She took out her phone and held it high—no signal. Feeling uneasy about this entire situation, she shoved the device into her pocket.

"Do you really think this is where they went?" asked Mason.

"There's nowhere else to go out here. Your dad would go where the people would be."

Mason stopped walking. "It doesn't look like there're any people here."

Haley's eyes roamed the barren street, lined with dilapidated buildings. The deafening silence hung heavy in the air. A musty odor mingled with the scent of decay, assaulting her nostrils. A chilling unease gripped her, seeping into her very core.

"Hey, mom! Look!" Mason tugged on her arm and pointed at a small cottage sitting at the end of a narrow street.

She couldn't see much, but she could see the radiant glow of a dim light flickering in a window.

"Let's go!" said Mason, taking a step forward.

"Wait!" shouted Haley, pulling him back. "What if they don't want to be bothered by uninvited guests?"

He shrugged. "We won't know unless we go find out. Besides, it's not like we have any other options. Dad and Riley could be there waiting for the tow truck."

He had a point. She nodded in agreement and followed her son down the dark street, toward the tiny house. Something about this entire situation set her nerves on fire. A vague memory scratched at the back of her mind, something primal, tucked away in a dark place. She shook her head and, once again, scolded herself for letting her fears get the best of her.

"It's just a tiny house, Haley," she muttered, as though merely saying those words would make it true.

The old cottage stood silently ahead, the light in the window glowing brighter. To their right stood a row of crumbling single-story homes with peeling paint, collapsed roofs and shattered windows. The pungent scent of decay hung heavy in the air. To their left, a sprawling cemetery stretched out, tombstones standing like sentinels of a distant past.

A sudden hoot pierced through the silence. Haley peered up to find a large barn owl staring down at her from the branch of a dead oak tree. A child giggled; she turned her head just in time to see a shadow duck behind a gravestone. Did she really see that? Was it another instance of her nerves getting the best of her? She continued along the street, keeping pace with her son, all the while watching the cemetery in her periphery for any sign of dancing shadows.

They stopped in front of the tiny home. Close up, it didn't appear as though anyone lived there. Sure, there was a flickering light in the window, but the house was just as desolate as the others.

The front door hung askew on a single rusty hinge. The windows were covered in rotting plywood, all except one that was nothing more than a gaping hole surrounded by shards of broken glass.

"Come on," said Mason as he moved down the walkway toward the front steps.

"I don't think we should go in," she said aloud.

He paused in front of the porch and cupped his hands around his mouth. "Hello!"

Nothing.

"Hello?"

The sound of a giggling child floated to Haley's ears. She turned her head and glimpsed a shadow moving behind the house.

"Let's go, Mase," she said.

"Hold on, I just wanna see if dad and Riley were here."

"We need to leave!" She reached out to grab hold of his arm, but he jerked away.

"You wait here," he said. "I'll go inside and look around. Maybe there's a phone."

"Mason, no! I'm your mother, now listen to me! Let's go!"

"I'll only take a second." Without another word, he climbed the steps to the front porch.

Before Haley could stop him, he had already stepped through the front door. Her maternal instinct overran her primal fear, she took the steps two at a time, storming through the door, only to run into Mason, who was frozen in place.

Her eyes scanned the room. Just as she thought, this was nothing more than an abandoned house. The smell of mold mingled with the stench of animal urine and feces. Tattered and torn wallpaper covered the walls. A single chair sat in the center of the room, a small table by its side had a kerosene lamp sitting atop it. The flickering flame cast an eerie glow, making it seem as though the shadows were dancing all around them. A message had been scrawled across the wall, "It's time to pay the Piper."

"That's creepy," he whispered.

"Yeah, it is. Now let's get out of here," said Haley.

"Who do you think lit the lamp?" asked Mason. He moved closer to the table.

"I don't know. I don't want to know. Let's go."

Mason didn't react to her pleas, instead he continued to the table where he picked up something at the base of the lamp.

"What the hell is that?" asked Haley.

He stepped closer to her, holding it up. "It looks like a stone." He flipped it around in his hand. "But it doesn't feel like any stone I've ever seen before. It's vibrating." He handed it over to her.

She rolled it around in her hand, running her thumb along the smooth surface. "This isn't stone," she said. Something was etched into it. She pulled out her phone and turned on the flashlight to get a better look. "It's bone," she whispered. "It's some sort of animal bone that someone carved this rune symbol into." A piercing stab erupted deep in her head, causing an intense pain. Unable to take it any longer, she dropped the trinket and collapsed to her knees, holding her head.

"Mom!" shouted Mason, repeatedly. "Mom, answer me!"

Her ears were ringing so loud, she could barely hear him. The pain in her head grew to a crescendo, then crested and finally waned, leaving her with a steady, dull throb. She peered up at her son, the look of worry on his face ignited her own fear.

"What was that?" asked Mason as he helped her back to her feet. "Are you okay?"

Haley nodded. "I'll be fine."

Mason bent down and picked up the rune. He studied the carving. "It kinda looks like a bowtie or a pointy infinity symbol. What do you think it means?"

"I don't know, honey." A blast of chilly air rushed past her, carrying, once again, the sound of a child giggling. She hugged herself. "Let's get out of here."

This time Mason didn't argue. He shoved the trinket into his pocket and followed Haley out of the house. Unwilling to walk past the cemetery again, she led them down the first side road, hoping that they were heading toward the center of the town.

CHAPTER 8

OUTSIDE THE SCHOOL, silence surrounded them. Riley's heart pounded fiercely in her chest, the rhythmic thumping echoing in her ears. Each breath she took was shallow and strained, her lungs struggling to draw in enough air. Dizziness threatened to overwhelm her. Leaning forward, she gripped her knees, feeling the cold sweat forming on her palms.

"Put your hands on your head and walk slowly," said Wade, his eyes scanning the area that surrounded them.

It took her a moment to process his words. She straightened her back and placed her hands atop her head, forcing herself to breathe slowly.

"It's okay," said Wade. "We're alright."

"What was that?" Just thinking about the demonic child sent an icy chill down her spine. Its image was seared into her mind with its haunting features, etching itself into her memory forever.

That laugh—it was the most evil laugh she had ever heard. The graffiti on the wall that said, It's time to pay the Piper. What the hell did that mean? Did they wander into a weird satanic cult nest? How does that explain that thing behind the bleachers?

Wade peered down at Riley. "You feeling better?"

She nodded, still unable to speak much.

He shook his head. "I have no idea what the hell that was." He stared up at the building. "I could have sworn we were following the sound of a crying child. But—"

"We have to go," said Riley. "We have to get out of this town now."

Her father pulled his phone from his pocket and held it up, the grimace on his face told her there was still no signal. Her heart sank, a dark cloud of helplessness descended upon her.

"Maybe we didn't see what we thought we saw," he said.

"You mean, we didn't just see a demon child with pitch black eyes and a mouth full of sharp pointy teeth?"

Wade chuckled nervously. "Well, when you put it that way." He peered into the open doorway to the high school. "Maybe we just think we saw it. Like a hallucination."

"Both of us? The exact same thing?"

He stared back at her.

"I know what I saw. And I know I was not hallucinating." Tears welled up in her eyes. "I wanna go home."

"Me too, Pixie." He wrapped his arms around her and waited until she stopped crying, then looked into her eyes. "You ready?"

She wiped her face with the sleeve of her shirt. "Where are we going? Back to the car?"

Wade shook his head. "I think the center of town is that way." He pointed.

"So? This town doesn't have anything we need. Please Dad, can we go back to the car?"

"We have to check if there's a signal or someone who can help while we're here," he insisted. "If we go back empty handed, I at least want to know without a doubt, there was nothing we could have done."

Riley hated the idea of going deeper into the creepy town, but she understood her father's point. "Dad. Do you think Mom and Mason are okay?"

"Yeah, I do," said Wade. "At least they're back at the wreck and not in this weird little place." He forced a smile. "Can you imagine how your mom would have reacted to what we just saw?"

"I think she'd be halfway to Dallas by now," chuckled Riley, thankful for the lighthearted moment.

"Come on, let's get this over with," he said.

The rest of the town was exactly as expected. Dark, desolate and creepy as hell. Even the air reeked of decay. Here and there Riley was sure she saw the shadows moving, but every time she turned to look directly at it, whatever it was would not be there.

Main street was a straight line of boarded up and partially decomposed buildings. As they strolled down the middle of the road, Riley tried to picture the town during its heyday, if there ever was one. Based on the size of the high school, there had to be a time when this creepy place was alive with people. What exactly happened to make all the residents disappear? Was it all at once, a cataclysmic event that pushed everyone out, or was it a slow, random death brought on by lack of opportunity?

They passed a two-story building, an old sign hung precariously from the stone edifice. Miller's Mercantile. She peered inside the dust covered windows, imagining how once upon a time, this store was probably the biggest store for miles around. They were probably the focal point for

Christmas. She tried to envision what the windows would have looked like all decked out for the holidays, but all she could see was rot, decay, and rats.

Inside the building, the sound of a loud crash echoed all around. Startled by the sudden sound, Riley's breath hitched in her throat. A high-pitched screech pierced the silence, accompanied by the distinct sound of rapid paws on concrete. Narrowly missing a collision with her, a large, black cat darted through a small hole in the wall with lightning speed.

She jumped out of its way, her heart racing in her chest as she watched the sleek animal disappear around a corner.

"Well," said Wade. "That's a positive sign."

"Why's that?"

"Animals won't stay in a place if they're in danger."

"Nice try," scoffed Riley. "Dad, please be honest. What do you think that thing was back there?"

He shrugged and sighed. "I wish I knew."

"Do you think that's what destroyed the town?"

"I don't think so. You have to remember, there are lots of towns like this all-over west Texas. Boomtowns that were built up but; once the mine or oil or whatever dried up, everyone left."

"I suppose," said Riley. "Do you think that's why that thing is back there? Like it's stuck here or something."

Wade stared down the street, his jaw flexing as though he were deep in thought. "Come on, let's keep looking. We're almost to the end of Main Street. I'm hoping there's a signal somewhere." He stopped abruptly and grabbed Riley's arm. "Do you see that?" he pointed.

She followed his gaze. At the end of the street, there stood a quaint little church, its bell tower reaching toward the sky. The building was the most well-maintained in the entire town. In fact, it looked downright out of place with its white exterior and fully intact stained-glass windows. From where they stood, she could see a warm, welcoming light flickering behind the colorful glass.

Wade walked toward the building, but Riley held firm. "Are we seriously going to go over there?"

"I don't see as we have any other choice," he replied.

"What if more of those things are in there?"

"In a church?" Wade ran his hand down his face. "If this is some sort of haunted town, I would think that a church would be the safest place to be. Besides, where there's light, there's people or a person. Probably some old priest. Which means we have a way to get some help." He tugged her arm. "Come on."

Riley's instincts were telling her to run, but she couldn't ignore the unwavering trust she had in her father. Maybe he was right. Maybe help was just a few yards away, waiting for them in that tiny, warmly lit church. After all, churches were consecrated land, weren't they? Nothing demonic could possibly enter. She was sure they would be safe within those walls.

CHAPTER 9

SOMETHING WAS BITING at the back of Haley's mind. Buried deep, beyond all conscious thought, she could sense it there, slowly picking its way forward like a worm, burrowing through the folds of her memories. The more she focused on it, the more fearful she became. Why? Why was all of this so familiar? She had never been to this town in her entire life. She was sure of that, a place like this would be remembered.

Mason led the way, his steps confident and purposeful, exuding a newfound sense of calm since the tiny cottage. It was almost as though he knew exactly where to go. She couldn't help but notice that he suddenly seemed unaffected by the palpable aura of unease that surrounded them. Maybe it was that rune he found.

A profound sense of dread washed over her as she recalled the rune. What kind of bone was it made from? What did the symbol mean? Was it some kind of curse? She wanted him to throw it away, but when she suggested he do just that, he refused. Something about that trinket had him enthralled.

A sharp, piercing pain erupted in her skull just behind her eyes. She cried out and stopped in her tracks, then rubbed her temples as a wave of nausea washed over her. Now was not the time for this. She mouthed a silent prayer for it not to be a migraine; she needed all her wits about her right now.

"You okay Mom?" asked Mason, his face a mask of concern.

Haley nodded her head. "I'll be fine. Just give me a minute." She sunk to the ground and leaned against a dead tree. Of course it would be dead, everything else in this godforsaken town was. A soft chuckle escaped her lips.

"What's so funny?" he asked.

"I was just thinking about how this is the perfect Halloween town. Don't ya think?"

A look of confusion swept across his face, followed by a warm smile. "I bet you regret all those horror movies now, don't you?"

"You have no idea, son."

They broke into laughter. It felt good—almost as though things weren't as bad as she imagined they were. No matter what had taken place so far, at least they had this moment of joy. She watched her son as he laughed with his perfect smile. A memory of the first time she ever heard him laugh surged forward. That sound, deeply embedded in her very soul was the most precious thing she would ever hear. It made her heart sing.

Haley's children were her world. Before she became pregnant, she never could imagine how deeply she would fall in love with her babies. If someone were to tell her when she was a teenager that there would come a day when she would be the doting mother of two beautiful babies, she would have laughed in their faces. When she was young, the last thing she ever wanted to be was a mother.

That is until she met Wade.

His family owned a big ranch on the edge of town. The oldest of three sons, he was blessed with the good looks and charisma that could charm any girl he wanted.

From the moment Haley laid eyes on him, she was in love. He consumed her thoughts day and night, his wild, dark brown hair and captivating smile haunting her every waking moment.

Waiting for the pain in her head to subside, she closed her eyes and basked in the memories of the time she met her true love.

CHAPTER 10

IN HER MIND, she could still picture that seedy little apartment in Dallas, with its worn-out furniture and the constant sound of the window bangers humming away.

The absence of a father figure was a constant void in Haley's life. Her attempts to learn about him were always met with a furious rant from her mother, followed by several days in a drunken stupor. Asking questions was something she learned to avoid, as it never yielded any useful information. So, young Haley relegated him to nothing but a name, printed indifferently on her birth certificate.

As for her mother, Sarah, support was in short supply. Years of alcohol, drugs, and abusive men had taken their toll. Working a minimum wage job at the dollar store occupied her days, while her evenings were characterized by a haze of drunkenness or drug-induced highs.

Sometime shortly after Haley's fifteenth birthday, her mother met the supposed love of her life. His name was Michael. To Haley, he was exactly like all the other low-life men her mother had brought home throughout the years.

Skinny and unremarkable, he was just another loser who moved in and became a burden.

At first, nothing much changed. That is, aside from the creepy feeling she would get whenever he was nearby. Every time she turned around, she would find him staring at her as though he were undressing her with his eyes. In response, she took to showering or coming out of her room only when necessary.

To say she hated her life would be an understatement. But there was nowhere else to go. She had no father, and according to Sarah, her grandparents wanted nothing to do with either of them.

Accepting her fate of facing life alone, she channeled her energy into school, envisioning a future where she could leave it all behind after graduation.

On the last day of her junior year, filled with excitement and a hopeful anticipation for the upcoming summer, Haley returned home to the sight of her mother and Michael in the disheveled living room.

As soon as she entered, Sarah rose to her feet and ran her hand down her puffy, red face. She had been crying.

This brought about no empathy from her daughter, she had seen this whole act before. These filthy men would come into their lives, upset things and watch young Haley as though she were a prey animal, then ultimately, they would tire of her mother and move on.

Throughout their stay, tears stained every moment, with arguments always trailing behind, followed by her mother's desperate pleas for forgiveness, even though she was not to blame. The cycle of idiocy seemed to have no end.

Sarah stepped aside and signaled for Haley to take a seat, but Haley refused.

"Okay then, we'll just jump right into it," said Sarah, wiping her hands on her thighs.

Michael leaned back in his chair and eyed Haley up and down in that lusty way of his, only this time he wore a smirk that she couldn't quite understand.

"Pack your things," blurted Sarah. "You're leaving tonight."

Shock washed over young Haley, leaving her speechless and frozen in place. To her surprise, her eyes welled up with hot tears that spilled down her cheeks. The lump in her throat made it difficult for her to speak coherently, causing her to struggle to form a sentence. What the hell did her mother mean? Go where? Overwhelmed with fear, Haley's voice quivered as she sobbed, "Momma, no! Please!"

Why was she begging? Hadn't she always dreamed of walking out that filthy door, never to return? She was finally getting what she had wanted since she became a conscious human being. She would be free.

But where was she to go? Was she to be homeless?

"Don't argue!" shouted Sarah. "Your grandparents are on their way. They'll be out front in half an hour, so get your shit packed and be ready at the curb."

As Haley absorbed the shocking news, an overwhelming sense of terror gripped her, leaving her anxious about the unknown that awaited her. With a steady diet of hatred and spine-chilling stories, Sarah had raised her to fear and despise the old couple. The only thing she knew about them was that they lived in a small town in north Texas, and that they were poor. Sarah was their only child, and they abused her every day of her life until she was finally old enough to leave them behind.

How could this happen? Was Haley really trading one problem for an even bigger one? As if her current existence wasn't already bad enough, she was about to discover just how much worse things could truly be.

She desperately tried to come up with an alternative, racking her brain for any possible solutions. Unfortunately, she had no real friends, in fact, she was a total loner at school. A loser that no one bothered to befriend. Was there a shelter she could go to? She had no idea.

In the end, she resigned herself to do what she had always done—exactly what Sarah told her to do.

With tears streaming down her cheeks, she packed her meager belongings, the weight of her emotions heavy in the air. Stepping out of her bedroom for the last time, she was met with her mother and Michael in the living room, completely absorbed in each other's company. Their laughter and affectionate kisses created an atmosphere that made her feel invisible. With a heavy heart, she wiped the tears from her face and walked outside to wait, feeling lonely and discarded.

Fed by the horror stories her mother raised her with, Haley's mind became a swirling vortex of terrifying scenarios, each one worse than the last. Consumed by her own despair, she didn't hear the car approaching until the blaring horn snapped her out of it.

The door to the silver vehicle swung open and an old man climbed out. He strolled up to Haley, his footsteps slow and deliberate, and paused, his gaze fixed on her.

With her hand raised to shield her eyes, she peered up at the mysterious figure that hovered above her. He didn't seem to be a monster; instead, his face wore a gentle smile that contrasted with the deep sorrow in his eyes. He held out a hand.

"Well, come on, young lady. No need to stay out here in the sun," he said with a kind voice.

Feeling a mix of hesitation and fear, she placed her hand in his and let him guide her toward the waiting vehicle.

From the passenger seat, a woman with thin, gray hair looked up at her, her eyes filled with a gentle kindness. Like the old man, her smile didn't quite reach her eyes.

The realization hit Haley as she settled into the back seat of their silver car—these were not terrifying creatures, but rather two individuals who had weathered devastating heartbreak.

As the car rolled away from the apartment building, Haley craned her neck to see if she could catch a glimpse of her mother's tear-filled eyes peering down at her. However, nothing of the sort occurred.

The ride through the city was silent. Haley welcomed this, relieved that she wouldn't have to stumble awkwardly through a conversation with the old couple in front of her.

As she peered out her window, the landscape changed dramatically from shabby, neglected apartment buildings and imposing skyscrapers to cozy, idyllic suburban residences; many of which were nearly as large as her entire apartment building. She couldn't help but wonder what it would be like to live in one of those houses. Were the people as happy as she imagined them to be? Or were they just as bent up and twisted inside as everyone she knew?

Gradually, the scenery changed to small rural towns, separated by miles of cow pastures and barbed wire fences.

Having never been to this part of the world, Haley was in awe over the sheer openness of it all. What were the people like who lived out here? Would they be as dismissive and cruel as the ones where she came from? Would they judge her thrift store clothes?

A small town came into view. She watched as they

drove down Main Street, lined with tiny shops. It was all so picturesque.

The car rolled to a stop in front of a tidy little house, nestled on a street filled with similar tiny, neat little homes. A small playground sat across the street. As Haley climbed out of the vehicle, the sound of children's laughter floated to her ears. Hardly able to recall the last time she heard such a joyful sound, she paused and stared, unable to pull her eyes away.

The air was filled with the scent of flowers, fresh cut grass and smoke from a bar-b-que. Haley closed her eyes and inhaled, filling her lungs.

"Come on dear," said the old woman with a soft, sweet voice. "Let's get you inside and settled. After supper, we can take a little walk and get you acquainted with the neighborhood."

Inside the tiny home, the air was filled with the same fresh scent as outside. She took a deep breath and noticed the absence of the usual stench of alcohol or stale cigarettes. Sheer white curtains swayed gracefully in the warm afternoon breeze. The moment she stepped into the cozy little kitchen; her senses were overwhelmed by the tantalizing scent of freshly baked apple pie.

"I made a pie for dessert," explained the old woman. Her face became serious. "Oh dear, it never occurred to me that you may not like apple pie." She peered at Haley with hopeful eyes.

"It's fine!" she blurted in response. "I love apple pie!"

The old woman smiled. "Well then, that's a good start." She leaned close and whispered conspiratorially, "At least now Amos will have to learn to share." She winked then turned around and led Haley down a narrow hallway.

The walls were adorned with a gallery of photographs.

It took Haley a moment to realize that most them were of her own mother. Shock washed over her as she gazed at the smiling childhood face of a woman she had always known as miserable. It occurred to her that she had never seen her mother smile in such a way. The woman she knew exuded an icy aura, her eyes hollowed and sunken from years of drug and alcohol abuse, cigarette smoking, and tumultuous relationships.

Her heart ached for the smiling, happy child that grew into a bright, joyful teenager right before her very eyes. What happened? She couldn't help but wonder, Why was this not the woman she knew?

The last image she saw was a photo of her mom as a carefree teenager, her smile brightening the frame, with the words 'Junior Year' boldly displayed at the bottom. Unable to reconcile the woman she knew with the cheerful teenager in the picture, Haley paused and studied it intently.

"Your room's right here," said the old woman. She gestured with her hand.

Haley walked slowly into the small bedroom, taking in the neat surroundings. A desk sat idle in the corner. Running her fingers across the top, she felt the excitement of having her own desk for the first time. There was even a chair! She spun it around. An empty cork board hung above the desk alongside a calendar.

She sauntered over to a cozy little window seat and gazed out through the sheer curtains at the park across the street, then spun around and made her way over to the bed where she let herself plop down upon the mattress. It was so soft, Haley wanted to lie down and feel the plush fabric against her body. Fighting back tears, she gazed up at the old woman and muttered, "Is this all mine?"

The old woman smiled and nodded her head. "Well, of course it is dear. You need a place to get some proper rest, as well as your own corner to do your schoolwork."

"Thank you," choked Haley, letting the words get stuck in her mouth as she realized she didn't quite know what to call this old woman.

Seeming to read her mind, the old woman responded with, "You can call me Letta, if you prefer. I won't ask you to call me Meemaw, since you've only just met me."

Haley smiled and nodded.

Letta sighed and glanced around the room. "Well then, I'll let you get settled in your new bedroom. Go ahead and unpack your belongings, it seems as though there's more than enough room in the closet." She stared down at Haley's pathetic backpack. "We don't have much, but I'll see to it that we get you some more things." She stepped out into the hallway. "Suppers in an hour. I hope you're hungry." Without waiting for a response, Letta pulled the door closed behind her, leaving Haley alone in her new room.

With a sense of immense relief, Haley settled onto the cozy mattress and stared up at the ceiling, feeling a wave of calm wash over her. As she closed her eyes, the sound of the children's laughter outside filled her ears, echoing with happiness.

That summer, Haley's life had changed in ways she had never imagined possible.

Amos and Letta were nothing like the ogres her momma had portrayed them to be, rather they were but two more people that Sarah abused and used, then tossed away when they were no longer of use to her. Just like Haley.

Her grandparents were kind and patient people. They

spent many hours taking her around the small town, proudly introducing her to anyone who would listen.

It was on one of those outings where Haley first laid eyes on Wade. She and her grandfather stopped by the local grocery store to pick up a few snack items as a treat. She rounded the corner and nearly collided with him. Tall and handsome, he smiled at her and quickly glanced away, only to turn his gaze back to her.

As a warm sensation rose from her belly up to her face, Haley found herself at a loss for words. Unable to speak, she gently brushed her hair behind her ear, offering a brief nod before deftly maneuvering around the young man.

While waiting at the checkout, her gaze landed on a sign that proudly declared, now hiring. With a huge smile, she turned to her grandfather and asked, "Do you think I should apply?"

Amos nodded. "Work is good for everyone. It's far better than sitting around with a couple of old folks all summer." He winked. "Besides, it'll give you a chance to get to know some of the local kids. Maybe even make a few friends before the new school year."

She needed no more prodding. Without hesitation, Haley filled out the application and handed it over to the clerk behind the service desk. With hope in her heart, she went home. Hardly an hour passed before the phone rang. It was the store manager asking her to come in for an interview.

Within a few days, she was hired and ready to show up for her first shift.

When she first started working at the store, the other teens were hesitant to warm up to her. Their demeanor made it clear that they were not open to welcoming anyone new. As for Wade, their conversations were few and far between. When he did come into contact with her, he would flash a fleeting smile and exchange polite greetings before swiftly moving on.

She worked as many hours as the store would give her, eventually saving up enough money to purchase her own car. Her grandpa helped her find the most reliable one, he even showed her how to change the oil, replace tires and put on new brakes. Elated and extremely proud of her accomplishment, Haley spent the afternoons when she wasn't working, driving around town.

Gradually, she struck up a friendship with Stephanie, one of her coworkers. Because of this friendship, one by one, the other teens became friends also, finally inviting her to join them at the lake.

Hoping that Wade would be among the attendees, she enthusiastically said yes.

On her way out the door that night, she told her grandparents that she was going to a movie with Steph. With cheerful waves, Amos and Letta told her to be home by midnight and sent her off.

Attending a lake party and joining other teenagers around a bonfire, was a completely new experience for Haley. Her entire body trembled with anxiety.

The parking lot was filled with vehicles. Feeling overwhelmed, she scanned the area, hoping to see Stephanie, sighing in relief as she laid eyes on her friend's car, followed by a rush of excitement when she realized that Wade's truck was parked right alongside. He was here! This was it. This was the opportunity she had been dreaming about. Finally, they would have the chance to talk freely, without their manager's prying gaze.

About what? Feeling suddenly nervous, she raked her brain, trying to come up with something to talk to him about that wouldn't make her sound stupid. He played football, but she knew nothing about the sport. His family owned a large ranch with horses and lots of cows; she, in contrast, had never seen either animal outside of television or books. Everything about his life was the polar opposite of hers.

Steph appeared out of nowhere, leaning into the driver's side window. "It's about time you got here," she said with a cheerful grin. "I was beginning to think you weren't gonna show." Stephanie pulled the door open. "Well, you gonna come on or what?"

"Okay, looks like everyone's here," announced Steph, as she dragged Haley along by her hand.

"Good," said Reed. "It's about time."

Haley recognized him as one of the stockers. He typically worked a different shift than her, so her interactions with him were limited, but she knew his type well. Athletic and charismatic, he was the kind of boy who took pride in sleeping with as many girls as possible, then bragging about it to his friends.

Reed whistled and waved his hands toward a gaggle of boys who were all standing beside the volleyball nets.

As soon as she saw Wade among the group, Haley's heart fluttered foolishly in her chest. Unable to calm herself and fearful she would look like an embarrassed fool, she glanced around the area and asked aloud, "Where are we gonna build the bonfire?"

"Not here, for one. Too many eyes," said Steph. "She grinned and pointed across the lake. "We're going over there."

"Is there a gravel road?" asked Haley nervously. "I don't think my car could make it on dirt without getting stuck."

"Come on," prodded Steph. "We're gonna ride together

in the trucks." She took hold of Haley's hand and pulled her toward Wade's truck.

Haley moved to climb inside the back seat, only to be stopped by Steph who guided her toward the front. With a gentle nudge, she pushed Haley inside first, forcing her to move along the seat until she stopped right beside Wade. Grinning from ear to ear, Steph climbed inside, effectively pinning Haley between them.

As Haley smiled at him and said hello, her cheeks grew warm with a rush of heat.

He nodded and flashed a perfect smile. "Glad you made it." Then he turned on his engine and leaned out of his window. "Come on losers," he called.

The rest of the group split up and loaded into the trucks. Leading the caravan, Wade drove out of the parking lot and turned onto the highway.

"I thought we were staying in the park," said Haley.

"The park won't let us have a bonfire," said Steph. "Which is why we go to the other side of the lake." She laughed. "Don't worry, we'll bring you back to your car when it's time to go home." Someone handed a joint to Steph, who took a hit then passed it over to Haley.

Never having smoked before, she stared at the joint, unsure of what to do.

"Go on," prodded Steph. "It won't bite you."

"At least take a hit or pass it back," said a boy in the back seat.

Painfully aware of all their eyes on her, Haley took a drag and inhaled, only to cough all the smoke out and wheeze as her lungs protested over the intrusion.

The truck turned down a narrow gravel road that soon gave way to an even more narrow lane with sparse gravel and a whole lot of dirt. As they weaved and bobbed their way around massive dips, she found herself jostled around so much she couldn't help but lean her entire body against Wade's. He didn't seem to mind, in fact, Haley could almost swear he leaned against her in response.

In a whirlwind of activity and enthusiastic shouts, they parked the vehicles and unloaded. Everyone seemed to know what they were doing, so Haley wandered around, trying not to look confused. Before long, they had a bonfire burning on the soft sandy shore, right along the water's edge.

Reed had shoved a cold beer in her hand. "Drink up," he said with a mischievous grin. "We got plenty."

Amid laughter and chatter, Haley watched the sunset as she reveled in a sense of belonging. The entire group treated her as though she were one of them. For the first time in her life, she felt as though she might belong—as though she finally had friends. The type of friends she had only ever seen on television.

As often as she could, she would talk to Wade, trying to learn as much as possible about him. The fact that none of the other boys made any effort to hit on her was obvious. She wondered if it was because of him.

The beers came one after the other, usually followed by a pipe, burning with weed or a paper rolled joint. The black sky above was adorned with a myriad of sparkling stars, creating a mesmerizing sight. Suddenly aware of the time, Haley glanced over at Steph and asked, "What time is it?"

"Ten O'clock," answered Wade. "What time you gotta be home?"

"Midnight," she croaked in response.

He smiled. "That's the time most of us have to be back. Don't worry, you'll make it."

A cool breeze rushed over the water, reminding her that

she had forgotten her jacket in her car. She leaned closer to the fire for warmth.

"Here," he said, as he removed his jacket and wrapped it around her shoulders.

Haley pulled it close to her body, breathing in deeply, allowing his intoxicating scent to fill her lungs. Across the fire, she saw Steph's beaming face, her smile stretching from ear to ear. After giving a quick nod of approval, her friend's attention shifted to Reed and the others.

Wade leaned so close that his lips brushed softly against her ear, sending a surge of heat throughout her body. "You wanna take a walk?" he whispered.

Ever since she first laid eyes on him, she had dreamt of this very moment. Her mouth suddenly dry, she swallowed and nodded.

They strolled along the beach, sharing small talk. He told her about his family, most of this information she already knew, but she pretended as though she had never heard it before.

On that sandy beach, where the warm sand shifted beneath their feet, he kissed her for the first time. With her senses buzzing, she couldn't resist his offer to join him in his truck.

That was the first time they made love. It was the first time she had ever been touched by a boy in that way.

Time seemed to slip through her fingers as the hour raced by. It didn't take long before a knock sounded at the window, and Reed's voice could be heard outside, shouting, "Hey!" Come on lovers, it's time to head out. I don't need to get in trouble for being late. My old man's got me on probation after we tore up the hay field last month."

After packing up, they put out the fire, then loaded into the trucks. Haley couldn't help but feel a pang of sadness as the vehicles leisurely maneuvered their way back down the narrow dirt road. She wished the night would never end. So much was left unsaid between her and Wade. She wanted to be with him forever.

Back in the parking lot, he held her hand as he walked her back over to her car where after opening her door for her, he kissed her goodnight.

As he walked away, he turned and smiled. "See you at work, Babe," he said, then spun around and returned to his truck where he helped a thoroughly drunken Reed get settled. A moment later, he swiftly rolled out of the parking lot, his truck lights disappearing from sight.

The entire drive home Haley replayed the evening over and over in her mind. As she climbed into bed, she pulled his jacket around her body and snuggled up, then drifted off to sleep.

Throughout the rest of the summer, things continued in the same manner. The group would meet up, drive to the spot along the lake, then she and Wade would wander off, make love, then rejoin the others. She was in bliss. Not only had she finally felt as though she belonged, but she had also found her true love.

CHAPTER 11

MASON WAITED PATIENTLY for his mother; his mind filled with curiosity as to why this place no longer gave him the uneasy feeling it once did. Back at the tiny house, something had shifted in him.

He shoved his hand in his pocket and brushed the rune with his fingertip. Ever since he found that tiny trinket, he was filled with a newfound sense of calm, as though there was nothing to worry about.

Scanning the empty street, he came to the realization that this creepy little town was mostly deserted, with only a few stray cats prowling the streets. The eerie atmosphere made it seem like a scene straight out of a horror movie. The only thing missing was the car full of young and stupid students. Then again, he and his family would qualify for that role.

No matter how hard he tried, he couldn't shake the feeling that someone was watching him—watching over him.

Maybe that was why it had been a while since he heard those eerie voices and giggles. He probably imagined all of that. After all, he hit his head hard in the crash. Come to think of it, his mom hit her head hard as well.

He glanced down at her, sitting on the ground with her eyes closed.

"You feeling better?" he asked.

She blinked then smiled up at him. "I think so. At least it feels like the headache is going away." Brushing her hands off on her thighs, she climbed to her feet. "You done messing around?" she said jokingly.

"I don't know," he replied. "I think I kinda like this dark and shadowy spot under the dead tree." He flashed a toothy grin.

Turning a corner, they suddenly found themselves standing in front of an abandoned high school, its windows shattered and graffiti covering the walls. For the first time since leaving the tiny cottage, a deep sense of foreboding descended upon him. He came to an abrupt halt and peered into the black abyss of the front door.

The sound of a child's laughter floated on the air.

"Did you hear that?" he asked his mom.

She stepped closer and took hold of his arm, gripping it tightly and pulling him close.

The same deep, soothing voice from earlier erupted in his ear, this time it was much closer. *"You have nothing to fear, no one can harm you."*

A sense of ease washed over him. Glancing around, Mason searched for any sign of the man who owned the voice, but the area was deserted. As far as he could tell, there were only two people in sight—him and his mother.

The sound of children's laughter grew louder, filling the air, multiplying and making it impossible for him to count how many voices there were.

In the shadows of the entrance, something moved,

capturing his full attention. Mason squinted his eyes, straining to see. He couldn't be sure if it was real or just a figment of his imagination, but he could swear he saw something rustling and expanding in the doorway. As he stared in disbelief, a dark figure materialized and gracefully stepped out from the depths of the shadows.

A child. A child with black eyes.

"You have nothing to fear," said the man's voice in his head. *"They will not harm you."*

The child made no effort to move beyond the threshold, instead it stood still, staring at him.

Before his eyes, another child appeared, standing just behind the first, followed by another and another. There must have been twenty of them all together. Mason stared in stunned silence.

The children chattered gleefully, *"He's pretty,"* said one.

Giggles.

"We want to keep him," said another.

"We cannot," said another. *"He is not ours to keep."*

Giggles.

"What does that mean?" shouted Mason, stunned that he said those words aloud. He glanced over at his mother who was staring at him with a terrified look on her face.

"What does what mean?" she asked. "Mason, what are you talking about?"

"It's okay, mom. I don't think they can hurt us."

"Who?" she asked with a trembling voice. "Who are you talking about?" She stared with a perplexed look on her face. "There's nothing there."

He moved his gaze back to the doorway.

The children were gone.

He ran his fingers through his hair, unsure if he should

describe what he saw. If his mom couldn't see it, maybe that was a good thing. He shook his head. "Nothing. It's nothing, mom."

She studied him for an awkwardly long period, then said, "That's it. Let's go. Now!" This time she wasn't asking.

The sound of a child's laughter floated to his ears.

His mother's grip tightened around his arm, causing a stab of pain. "I said let's go!" she hissed.

As Haley shoved him forward, Mason peered over his shoulder and saw a black-eyed child in a window. Smiling eerily, she waved at him, then disappeared.

By the time they reached the end of the street, there was no sign of the children at all.

CHAPTER 12

RILEY STOOD BACK as her father pushed open the massive church doors. With a sound resembling a tortured cry, the rusty metal hinges protested against being opened. Inside, the air was filled with the heavy scent of incense, mingling with the lingering smell of dust and mold. She wrinkled her nose, trying to suppress a sneeze that tickled her senses.

Wade whistled softly. "Well, this is weird," he said aloud, taking a step forward.

"Should we be doing this?" asked Riley, more than a little nervous. "Maybe it's not safe to go in."

"If we aren't safe in a church, where would we be?"

Unable to come up with a counterargument, she sighed and followed her father into the building.

The scent of burning wax filled the air as the candles in the tall candelabras cast a soft, comforting light around the sanctuary. Silent and empty, wooden pews lined the narrow aisle on both sides. As she looked up, the wooden ceiling with its worn out planks, soared overhead. Much to her surprise, the stained glass windows were intact.

Wade stepped up on the altar and ran his finger along the top of the podium. He glanced up at Riley and said, "No dust. Someone takes good care of this place." He scanned the empty chapel.

"Why would they leave these candles lit like this?" asked Riley.

"Either they had to leave in a hurry, or they always leave them lit so worshippers can come and pray any time."

As her gazed around the altar, a chill ran down Riley's spine upon noticing the cross looming ominously at the back, turned upside down. A knot of unease formed in the pit of her stomach. "Pray to who?" she whispered, her voice trembling, as she pointed behind her father.

Wade followed her gaze and gasped. He cleared his throat and said, "It must have fallen over."

Riley cautiously scanned the entire chamber, her eyes darting from one corner to another, absorbing every detail of the eerie sight before her for the first time. The stained-glass windows, she once thought were depictions of the story of Christ, now transformed into grotesque scenes of demonic revelry. She approached the nearest one, her footsteps echoing softly on the cold stone floor, and examined the intricate details.

A profound sense of dread engulfed her, as if icy fingers wrapped around her soul, causing her skin to prickle. Her heartbeat quickened, resonating loudly in her ears, mimicking the frantic rhythm of a small prey animal ensnared in the clutches of a formidable predator.

"Dad, we should leave. Now."

With hardly another word, Wade stepped away from the altar and came up alongside her. He studied the story depicted in the stained glass, then took hold of Riley's hand and said, "Let's go."

Moving rapidly, they made their way to the doorway.

CHAPTER 13

THE SOUND of their footsteps bouncing off the abandoned buildings was almost comforting to Mason. His mind replayed the image of the children at the high school, followed by the calming voice of the strange man. He shoved his hand into his pocket and ran his finger over the rune.

"Do you see that?" asked Haley as she gently tapped his arm. She pointed to the end of the street.

Mason followed her gaze. "Is that light?"

She nodded. "It is."

"From what?" He stared at the warm glow emanating from something just around the corner.

His mom shrugged. "Your dad and Riley might be up there."

"What makes you say that?"

"It only makes sense. If there's a light, there's people."

He glanced over at his mother. "The little house back there didn't have anyone in it. What if this one doesn't either?"

Haley nervously scanned the darkness that surrounded them. "Its gotta be better than this."

Once again, Mason studied the warm, glowing light at the corner. "Do you think that's where the owner of the little house went?"

"It's possible. Maybe that's where everyone in the town is."

"Yeah. But what sort of animal are they sacrificing?"

She shoved him gently. "Don't say that!"

A sharp gust of wind howled through the air, causing a momentary shiver to crawl down Mason's spine. He squinted ahead at the distant glow. The comforting light against the darkness beckoned him with its golden hue, promising safety and refuge.

The reassuring sensation of the rune against his fingertip, made it so he felt no fear or apprehension. How was this even possible? He had never been a religious person. His family hadn't stepped foot inside a church in years.

As they approached the corner, he was overwhelmed with a deep need to get to wherever it was that the light emanated from, fueled by the hope that perhaps they would find some answers there.

At the corner, they paused and stared up ahead. The emptiness of the street was broken only by the presence of a lone building, standing as a silent sentinel. A church. The door stood wide open, revealing the warm, inviting light that pierced through the darkness like a fiery blade.

Mason took a step forward, but Haley grabbed him by the arm.

She stared up at the building with a strange look in her eyes.

"You okay?"

She nodded slowly and swallowed. "It's a church. You know, hallowed ground and all. We'll be fine in there."

"What if it ain't that kind of church?" asked Mason, jokingly.

His mom scoffed. "What other kind of church is there?" She took a step forward. "Come on. There's only one way to find out."

Clenching the rune tightly in his hand, Mason followed his mother. The church was now just a few yards ahead of them. As he peered inside, he could see shadows moving. Subtle and barely noticeable, it appeared as though there was someone or something there.

In the middle of the road, he came to a stop and looked up at the wide stone steps. The warm glow from ahead beckoned him, but a faint, lingering sense of foreboding gripped him tightly.

The shadows shifted, this time, they were plainly visible; he didn't imagine them.

As he watched intently, they slowly transformed into figures, their silhouettes standing tall with their backs turned towards the blinding light, leaving Mason unable to identify who or what they were.

"There you are!" shouted his mother.

Mason lifted his hand above his eyes and squinted. It was at that moment that he realized the two figures standing in the doorway were none other than his father and sister. Rather than feeling relieved, a strange unease crept over him, creating a deep sense of dread.

CHAPTER 14

RILEY'S HEART swelled with relief at the sight of her mother and brother.

"How'd you find us?" asked Wade.

Climbing the stairs, Haley reached her husband's side and came to a stop. She planted a kiss on his cheek, then replied, "We couldn't stay at the wreck any longer." She wrapped her arms around Riley and gave her a hug. "It was way too creepy." She glanced around at the abandoned town. "So, we decided to see if we couldn't run into you somewhere down the road. We ended up in this place."

"Creepy, huh?" said Riley.

"You don't even know the half of it," said her mom. She nodded toward Mason. "Show her what you found."

Riley watched as her brother pulled something from his pocket and handed it over to her. Rolling the talisman around in her hand, her fingers traced the strange symbol carved into the surface. "Where'd you find this?"

Mason pointed back down a dark side street. "At an old house back there. It was all lit up like someone was in it just before we arrived."

"Did you see anyone?" asked Wade.

"It was weird," said Haley. "No one was around, but someone had lit one of those old-time oil lamps. How about you? Did you see anyone? Anything?"

While Wade recounted their stroll through the town, Riley carefully examined the intricate details of the talisman in her hand. She wasn't typically a spiritual sort of person, but she swore she could feel some sort of vibration emanating from the item. She turned to Mason. "What do you think it's made from?"

"Bone," replied her brother, his voice almost excited as he said the word.

Suddenly, the trinket felt grimy and repulsive in her hand. She gave it back to Mason. "Ew, why are you keeping it?"

He shoved it back in his pocket and shrugged. "I don't know, it just feels right to hold on to it."

"This place isn't right," said Haley. "We need to go."

For the first time since seeing her mother and brother, Riley noticed a strange undertone to her mom's voice—a subtle quiver that betrayed her fear. Her mother was afraid of this place. Riley could hardly disagree, something about this whole circumstance felt manipulated. It was almost as though this place had been waiting for them to arrive.

Suddenly, the quiet of the night was shattered by the sound of someone whistling, coming from a dark side street. The rhythmic sound of footsteps on the asphalt harmonized with the creepy tune.

Riley felt a surge of fear deep within her, rendering her motionless and speechless, her eyes fixed in terror on the shadow leisurely advancing nearby.

Against the radiant glow of the church, the shadow

grew shorter, disappearing altogether as the man who cast it, strolled toward them at a leisurely pace.

Riley's gaze shifted between her parents, who mirrored her own astonishment as they watched the strange man make his way to the church. Instinctively, she inched closer to her father.

With a mouth full of dazzling, pristine teeth, the man paused at the bottom of the steps and flashed a broad, confident grin. Against his smooth, pale complexion, his eyes gleamed like fiery red rubies. As he raked his fingers through his thick, black hair, his gaze slowly traveled across each member of the family until it settled on Haley.

"It's so wonderful to see you again, my dear," he said with a subtle nod.

CHAPTER 15

AS HALEY LAID eyes on the man standing before them, a wave of nausea threatened to overwhelm her. Memories long forgotten surged forth from the depths of her mind, shaking the ground beneath her with an unstoppable force. In its wake, the despicable truth lay bare.

A wave of panic engulfed her, causing her chest to tighten as if caught in a whirlwind. The world spun around her like a malevolent tornado, revealing the true identity of the man standing before them and the purpose of their presence in this location. Overwhelmed, she leaned over, retching uncontrollably.

Wade reached out to steady her, but she shoved him away.

Sporting a wicked grin, Mephistopheles stood patiently, his red eyes never leaving her as he waited. He ascended the steps with deliberate slowness, finally halting inches away from her. With a blend of amusement and intense revulsion, he gazed down at her. "This part always hurts a little," he said. "You'll find if you simply breathe through it, equilibrium will soon be established."

All around her Haley could hear the sounds of her family's voices as they asked questions in a feeble attempt to make sense of what was going on. Unable to discern their words, she found herself lost in a sea of memories from the past.

As Autumn made its presence known, Haley prepared for her senior year. For the first time, she wasn't apprehensive, as she was entering a new school with an entire circle of friends. This was going to be the best year of her life.

Unfortunately, Wade was a full year older than her, and rather than joining her at high school, he was heading off to his first year of college.

She did her best not to think of it, but deep down, this scared her. How was she going to pass the days between visits? What if he met someone else?

Luckily for her, she had friends to keep her company and work to occupy her time. She decided that she wanted to go to college, envisioning a future where she and Wade could share a cozy apartment. With that goal in mind, she took on a second job and worked tirelessly to build up her savings.

Due to the need to study, Wade didn't come home to

visit. In fact, he was so busy with his classes, he hardly took the time to talk over the phone. But Haley knew she would see him when he returned home for Thanksgiving.

A few days before the holiday, he called her to tell her he wouldn't be coming home. He explained his grades weren't too great, so his parents decided it was best if he stayed on campus and spent the extra time studying.

Initially feeling upset over the news, she pushed aside her feelings of distrust. After all, Wade wasn't like that.

"That's okay," she said, doing her best to mask her sadness. "We can make up for it over Christmas break."

"We'll see," he replied with a distant tone.

Thanksgiving came and went, a blur of heavy food, football on the television, and a deep sense of depression.

Over the course of the following weeks, she spent her days in school, afternoons working and her weekends partying with her friends. The lack of communication from Wade left her feeling disconnected and longing for his presence. She began to wonder if something was wrong.

One night, in a drunken state, Reed tried to kiss her. She shoved him away.

"What? Do you think you're something special?" he asked mockingly.

"Wade wouldn't appreciate what you just tried to do," she said.

Reed shook his head and laughed. "Oh, Haley, you really are thick, aren't you? Do you honestly believe you and Wade are a thing? That you were anything more than someone to fuck before he headed off to college?" He moved close enough to leer over her. "Think about it Haley." He tapped the side of his head. "The whole time you two were screwing in the back seat of his truck, did he ever take you home to meet his parents? Well? Did he?"

Haley struggled to find words to counter his tirade, but her voice failed her, leaving her motionless as she absorbed his relentless outburst.

Reed continued, "Quit being a fool and move on. There ain't nothing to hang on to. He's got a serious girlfriend." A wicked grin played across his lips. "One that he already brought home to meet his whole family."

She shook her head, refusing to believe him.

"It's true," pressed Reed. "I met her at Thanksgiving."

The weight of that last sentence landed on her like a sucker punch. Tears streamed down her cheeks as she spun around, taking in the solemn expressions on her friend's faces.

They knew. They all knew.

She took off, running through the woods sobbing, desperate to make her way back to her car. The entire drive home, Reed's words churned in her head. She spent the rest of the weekend alone, in her bedroom, staring up at the ceiling, heartbroken and lonely.

The following Monday at school, it was painfully clear that not only had the love of her life abandoned her, but all her friends had followed suit. They went to great lengths to steer clear of her in the halls, and at lunch, they left her to sit alone.

Once again, she found herself on the fringes, feeling like an outsider—the social pariah that everyone avoided.

Distraught and filled with anger, her hatred grew like a storm brewing, ready to unleash its fury. Night after night, she would numb herself with alcohol, drinking until she lost all sense of awareness.

It was during one of these binges that her rage began to simmer and eventually exploded. Fueled by liquid courage, she bravely drove to his college to confront him.

With her heart still racing, she sat in the parking lot of his dorm, trying to regain composure as she gently wiped away the tears staining her face. She wavered for almost thirty minutes, debating whether to enter the building or retreat home. Eventually, she resolved it was time to face the unknown. Better that she heard it directly from him.

She climbed out of her car and walked toward the building. Stepping inside, she was instantly hit with the realization that she had no clue which room was his amidst the maze of doors and hallways. He had never told her, and she had never visited before. Did he plan it this way all along?

She asked a young man where she could find a directory, he instead helped her to find Wade's room.

Adjusting her clothes and running her fingers through her hair, she stood at the door and took a deep breath before knocking.

Tap, tap, tap.

The door flung open, and Haley found herself staring at the face of a young woman with rosy cheeks, long, blonde hair and sparkling blue eyes. In a moment of awkward confusion, they locked eyes with each other, unsure of what to say or do, until Wade suddenly appeared. As soon as he laid eyes on Haley, a look of irritation washed over his face. He let out a heavy sigh before whispering something to the other girl, then exited the room, gently shutting the door behind him.

"What are you doing here?" he asked.

Still reeling from the shock of seeing her fears proven true, Haley struggled to put together words. "I-I wanted to talk to you."

Wade grabbed her by the arm, pulled her down the stairs and out of the building. "What could possibly be so important that you drive all the way out here?"

"Who is that girl?" she blurted. "Are you cheating on me?"

He sighed and shook his head. "Stop being so thick! I'm not cheating on you, because there is no us!" He stepped back and stared at her with cold eyes. "There never was."

Haley felt as though she had been struck across the face with a lead pipe. Her heart shattered into a million pieces in her chest. Tears exploded from her eyes as she struggled to comprehend what he was saying.

"Look Haley," he said with an ice-cold tone. "We had sex. We hung out during the summer and fucked. That's it. There never was anything more to it." He pointed to the parking lot. "Go home!"

"But—," she sputtered.

"There is no but! There is no us! There never was! Go home!" Once again, he directed his finger at the parking lot. "And leave me the fuck alone!" Without another word, he spun around and stormed back into the dorm, leaving Haley alone as she struggled to understand all that had just happened.

Reed's taunting voice and laughter echoed in her mind.

Heartbroken and hysterical, she raced out of the parking lot and drove into the night, her mind consumed by vivid memories of their time together, now tainted by Wade's cruel words.

She pressed the gas pedal to the floor, her long hair whipping around her face, sticking to her tear-stained skin. Setting her sights on a large tree that sat along a four-way intersection, she inhaled deeply, and closed her eyes, waiting for impact.

A voice suddenly spoke from behind her, sending a shiver down her spine as it whispered in her head, *"It doesn't have to be this way."*

With a sudden jolt, the steering wheel slipped from her grasp as an unseen presence gently guided her vehicle to a halt at the side of the road.

"Who said that?" she yelled.

Silence.

Haley scanned the backseat of her car, her eyes darting from side to side, but there was no sign of anyone.

"I did," said the voice again, smooth as silk, now coming from right outside her car.

As she turned her head, her eyes met those of a mysterious, yet strangely attractive man. His blood-red eyes locked onto her, and a mischievous grin danced on the edges of his lips as he gazed down at her. "And I meant it. It doesn't have to be this way."

"Who are you?"

He reached out his hand. "My name is Les. I'm here to make you an offer of a lifetime," he said with a gleam in his eye.

CHAPTER 16

RILEY AVERTED her gaze from the mysterious man and shifted her attention to her mom, shocked by the peculiar expression on her face.

"Who are you?" demanded Wade.

The man didn't respond.

There was no response from Haley, either; she simply stood there, wide-eyed and shocked, mouth gaping open.

"Mom?" prodded Riley. When no answer came, she turned back to the strange man.

Their eyes met, and Riley felt a sudden chill crawl down her back, sending a shiver throughout her entire body. A wave of primal terror engulfed her, causing her leg muscles to twitch in response. As she stood frozen in fear, her inner voice grew louder, screaming at her to run for her life. Heart fluttering in panic inside her chest, she turned to her father, who was moving closer to the strange man.

"I'm not gonna ask you again. Who are you?" he boomed.

"Oh," said the stranger. "Allow me to introduce myself." He held his slender hand out toward him.

When Wade made no move to take it, the stranger regarded him with calculating eyes as though he were sizing him up. Despite his lips spreading into a wide grin, his red eyes remained cold and unfeeling. "You can call me Les. I've been known by many names. The most common of which is Mephistopheles."

A gasp escaped Haley's lips, her hand shooting up to protect her throat.

Riley shuddered, fully aware that the man wasn't lying. She turned to Mason, who was standing there, watching the entire exchange with the strangest look on his face.

"Bullshit!" shouted Wade. He stepped closer to Les.

The creepy smile on Les's lips vanished, replaced by a scornful sneer.

"Save the bravado," he said dismissively. "My business is not with you." He slid his gaze over to Riley, where he stared for an uncomfortably long period, then he tilted his head toward Haley.

"No!" shouted Haley. She flung herself at Les with such speed that even Wade could not stop her. With hands outstretched into claws, she slashed at the stranger's face as if she wanted to tear his eyes out.

With a wave of his hand, Les forced Haley to her knees on the ground before him.

Bursting into action, Wade charged forward.

Les shifted his gaze, and, with a quick jerk of his head, he sent Wade flying. The sound of his body crashing down upon the asphalt echoed through the deserted street.

"Dad!" shouted Riley and Mason in unison.

"Silence!" boomed the man. "That's enough playing around." He snapped his fingers.

The air grew icy cold.

All around them the shadows gathered and grew. As

Riley watched in terror, children emerged from the darkness, encircling them until there was nowhere to go. Their eyes, black as coal, their skin the palest of white. They said nothing, standing completely still as though they were waiting for a cue from Les.

He leaned over Haley. "It's time."

"No! Please!" she sobbed, making no effort to rise to her feet. She shook her head. "Don't do this."

Wade made another effort to tackle Les, only to be deflected once again.

"If you value your life," warned Les. "You won't try that again." He turned his attention to Riley and took one step forward.

"No!" shouted Haley. "I won't let you!"

"Ah, my dear, it's far too late to rescind our agreement," said Les. "The time has come to pay the price." He let out an eerie chuckle. "To pay the Piper—if you will."

"What's he talking about Haley?" shouted Wade.

Les waved his hand, moving Haley out of his path as though she were nothing more than a bothersome piece of lint. He strolled over to Wade and leaned over him. "I suppose you deserve an explanation."

"Please!" begged Haley. "No!"

"Do you want to tell him?" asked Les. "Or should I?"

Haley whimpered, her head shaking back and forth as she muttered under her breath.

"Alright then," sighed Les. "Looks like it's on me." He glared at Wade. "Nineteen years ago, Haley and I entered into an agreement. One that would alter the trajectory of both her life and yours."

Fear seeped into every fiber of her being. Riley moved closer to Mason who wrapped his arm protectively around her shoulder. It did little to calm her trembling body.

"What is he talking about Haley?" asked Wade, in a defeated tone that Riley had never heard before.

"Don't listen to him," sobbed Haley. "He's lying!"

"Now why would I do that?" asked Les. "There's no benefit to me whatsoever."

Wade stared up at Les. "What was this deal?"

"I thought you'd never ask," replied Les, grinning like a gleeful child who was about to divulge a great secret.

The children inched forward, their small footsteps echoing as they closed the circle tighter around them.

Les crouched down, so that he was eye level with Wade. "You were a cold-hearted young man, my friend. Toying with the hearts of vulnerable young ladies." He reached out a slender finger and touched Wade on the forehead. "Maybe this will help you recall."

Wade cried out, raising his hands to his head as though he were in pain.

"Stop it!" shouted Haley.

Les stepped back, allowing Wade to rise to his feet.

He turned to Haley. "We broke up," he said as though he were remembering for the first time. "We broke up, and I had a new girlfriend. Becca." His lips curled into a mournful smile. "I loved her so much. I wanted to marry her. Then one night, she died in a freak accident with a drunk driver." Tears streamed from his eyes. "It was New Year's Eve, just a couple of weeks after you visited the dorm."

He stared forward with glassy eyes. "I was devastated. I took the next semester off and went home. You were there. You were always right there. We slept together—and then you were pregnant."

Wade glanced over at Riley and Mason. "I can't believe I forgot all of this. It's like an entire part of my life was hidden this whole time." He pinched the tears from his eyes and glared at Haley. "Why? Why did you do this?"

Haley's body trembled as she let out heart-wrenching sobs, her head shaking in denial.

"She did what most women would do when the love of their life turns out to be a scoundrel," said Les. "She made a bargain."

Haley rose to her feet and closed the distance between her and Wade. Sputtering and sobbing she said, "It wasn't like that. I loved you. I still love you. I didn't have a choice. You have to understand!" She reached out for him, but he shoved her away.

"Lies! All lies!" shouted Wade, backing away from her.

Haley rounded on Les, her eyes blazing with anger. She ran for him once again as she screamed, "You were supposed to collect your payment sooner! It was supposed to be a baby! Why are you doing this now?"

"Oh Haley," said Les. "Don't you understand, it isn't a sacrifice if it doesn't hurt. It's far more painful when you've had eighteen years together." He slid his gaze up the stairs, settling directly upon Riley.

"Riley! Mason! Run!" shouted Wade as he launched at Les. Before he could even make contact, Les effortlessly tossed him several yards away. He landed right in front of the demonic children, who immediately pounced upon him, holding him down. Several more children grabbed hold of Haley, pinning her down as well.

Fear squeezed Riley's chest like a vice, making it hard for her to breathe. She tried to move, but her legs wouldn't do as she willed.

Mason shoved her behind him and stood firm with his chest out, fists at the ready. "Get back!"

Stepping forward with an eerie glare, Les paused right

in front of Mason. Something in his face shifted, almost as though it grew softer as he stared at her brother. "This is not your fight, boy. Someone has plans for you." He flicked his hand, flinging Mason across the steps.

"Please! Take me!" begged Wade. "Leave her alone!"

More children appeared, closing the circle around Riley.

"She's ours!"

"Come play with us."

"Pretty girl."

Tears streaming down her cheeks, she begged, "Please, no." But she knew it was of no use.

Les stepped back, giving the children the ability to close in around her.

"Momma?" sobbed Riley. "Daddy? Please help me."

Beyond the throng of the black-eyed children, Riley could hear her family plead and beg. The tiny demons closed in all around her until all she could hear was their eerie chatter. Alone and terrified, she felt the first set of fingers lash out at her body. Like tiny knives, the nails bit through her clothes, tearing her flesh. She cried out in pain.

CHAPTER 17

RILEY'S PIERCING screams echoed through the stillness of the night, bouncing off of the motionless buildings that bore witness to the unfolding terror. The air was heavy with the metallic scent of blood and the sound of tearing fabric as the children viciously attacked her, leaving a gruesome mess in their wake.

At the bottom of the steps, Mason's parents let out piercing screams and begged for mercy, but their pleas went unanswered.

Haley cried out in rage, then aimed the handgun. Struggling against the grip of the children, she pulled the trigger. Bang! Bang! Bang!

In rapid succession, shots were fired, one, two, three, four, yet none of it mattered. His mother may as well have been firing blanks.

Mason wanted to move, but he could only stand there and stare. A soft, gentle voice whispered in his mind, *"Be calm, my young friend. The events of this night had been coded long before you were born. There's nothing you can do to alter the outcome."*

Riley's screams faded, replaced by the unsettling sound of the children devouring her remains.

Time stopped, or at least it seemed as though it did. The still, calm voice was silent, as though whoever were behind it was also watching along with Mason and his parents.

The children moved away, disappearing into the shadows, like ghosts retreating to their haunted realm.

Collapsing to his knees, Mason's eyes fell upon the pool of blood and tattered clothes that was all that remained of his sister.

"All lies!" cried his father.

Mason glanced up to see Wade standing with slumped shoulders. Haley, on her knees and sobbing, seemed completely unaware of her surroundings.

"Why would you do this?" said Wade, glaring at her. "What kind of monster are you?"

Haley ignored him, instead she leaped to her feet and launched toward Les, inadvertently kicking the gun across the ground, closer to Wade. "You've ruined everything!"

With a careless wave of his hand, Les sent her careening through the air, landing on the pavement with a solid oof. She climbed to her feet and charged at him again, only to have him do it again, this time landing at Wade's feet.

As she peered up at her husband, a look of stark terror washed over her face. She held up her hands and begged, "No. Please! Wade! I did it for—"

Bang!

Her face went slack. A tiny red spot materialized in the center of her forehead, then a thin wisp of smoke curled upwards from the wound, as if her soul was escaping her body. She crumpled to the ground.

"Mom!" screamed Mason. Running down the steps, he skidded and slipped before falling to his knees, cradling his lifeless mother in his arms. Tears streaming down his face, he looked up at his father.

With a calm and serene expression, Wade gazed down at his son. His face wet with tears, he swallowed then said, "I'm so sorry, son." Then he put the barrel of the gun between his lips.

"No!" screamed Mason.

Bang!

As Mason watched his father's body collapse to the ground, a deafening ring filled his ears, drowning out all other sounds.

His anguished cries echoed through the air as he rocked back and forth. His whole family was gone. Closing his eyes tightly offered no relief as the nightmare continued to unfold, repeating itself in his mind like a terrifying movie on a loop. Through hot tears, he peered up at Les. "Well? What are you waiting for?" He rose to his feet and stood with his arms down and chest out. "Kill me!"

The strange man's face contorted, revealing a fleeting expression of pity. With a shake of his head and a cluck of his tongue, he stepped closer.

"My young friend, death is not in the cards for you tonight."

Mason's eyes swept across the ground until it settled on the gun, clenched in his father's lifeless hand. He reached down and pried it from Wade's fingers, then raised the weapon under his chin. As the barrel pressed against his skin, he could feel its lingering warmth. He closed his eyes.

Click.

Nothing.

Click.

Once again, nothing.

Click, click, click.

Opening his eyes, he let out a piercing scream.

With his arm outreached, Les stepped closer to him.

Mason aimed the gun at the strange man and pulled the trigger.

Bang!

Les stopped in his tracks, then with that creepy smirk on his face, he retrieved the bullet from his chest and held it up. "Now, that's not very nice of you, is it?" he said, then he tossed the bullet to the ground and poked his finger through the hole in his vest. "I rather liked this suit."

Mason stood trembling, his mind a jumbled mess, unable to make sense of what he had just witnessed. He swallowed against the lump in his throat and said, "You're a crossroad demon, right?"

His deep-red eyes glistening in the moonlight, Les nodded.

"I wanna make a bargain!" shouted Mason. "Take my soul! I give it to you right now! In exchange, you bring them all back!"

"I'm afraid it doesn't work that way my young friend."

"Why not?" demanded Mason. "You collect souls, I'm giving you mine! A deal is a deal."

"And a deal, once agreed upon, cannot be undone," said Les. "The payment cannot be substituted for anything." He stepped closer and placed a hand on Mason's shoulder. "I told you earlier, my young friend, you have a destiny."

Mason shoved him away. "Fuck you!" he shouted. "Stop talking in circles! I don't want your destiny! I want to die!"

"This is not an offer that can be made," whispered the smooth voice.

Mason's body twisted in a whirlwind of anxiety, his eyes darting from shadow to shadow, his mind consumed by the ghostly voice that had haunted him relentlessly.

"Show yourself! Goddammit!" he shouted. "Stop hiding behind whatever the hell it is you're hiding behind. If you've got something to say, say it to me face to face!"

Once again, Mason scanned the abandoned street. Nothing. Despair washed over him, wiping away any sense of resolve he had. He collapsed to his knees in front of the bodies of his dead parents. His whole life was a lie. The woman he thought his mother was, was nothing more than an act. Her lies brought them to this place. Her lies set him on a path in life where he was now condemned to relive this nightmare repeatedly. How was he ever going to live after this?

Every time he blinked, he saw the haunting images of all that had taken place, play out on a loop.

"I don't want to live anymore," sobbed Mason.

"I can offer you a reprieve," said the calm voice. *"A lifetime free of this horror, where you live out all your dreams. No pain, no heartache, and no memory of this night. In its place, fame, fortune, the love and adoration of millions of people and any woman you desire."*

"What do I need to do?" asked Mason.

"Invite me in," said the voice. *"Allow me to reside within your body."*

"Are you a demon?"

A soft chuckle reached his ears followed by a gentle sigh.

"My young friend, if that is the title you choose to use, then so be it. I am but an ageless being whose time has come once again. Through you, we can both achieve our goals."

"What's your name?"

"People have known me for centuries by the name Ratten Koenig, or rather in English, the Rat King. You may have

heard of me as a child as The Pied Piper. You may call me Ten."

Mason inhaled. "Okay, Ten. What happens if I refuse your offer?

"Then you shall leave here and live out the rest of your life in misery and heartache."

He mulled those words over. The thought of reliving the events of this night for the rest of his life was terrifying. "How do I know you're telling the truth? What if you're lying to me, setting me up the way Les did to my mom?"

"That is not my way," replied Ten. *"I have no intention of deceiving you. I merely want to share the space that you hold."*

"You mean possess me."

"As I stated, I have no desire to possess, I merely wish to share. Two separate spirits—one body."

Mason could feel the presence move closer to him. There was something about it that filled him with a deep sense of tranquility, causing his heartache to fade. "Can you do what you promise? Can you make me forget?"

"I can," replied Ten confidently.

"Will it hurt?"

"It will not. You will fall asleep. And when you awaken, it will be as though I have always been with you. I will be a part of you, and we will do great things together."

"I don't care about that," said Mason.

"For now, you don't. That's because the pain is still within you. Once it's gone, you will see the greatness that awaits and you will be overjoyed."

Mason stared down at his father's body. "I don't want to forget them."

"Then you will not. I will craft a story that will set your mind at ease."

He mulled over the offer, knowing he didn't want to remember anything that happened this night. There was no way he could live with the knowledge. He stood up and wiped the snot from his face. "Okay," he said with a nod of his head. "I give you permission." He held up his hand. "But on one condition."

"Name it child."

"I want my sister back."

"My boy, this is not possible."

"Then there's no deal!" he shouted. "You supposedly can do anything. Do this!"

The demon pulled back. Mason got the distinct sense that it was pondering his offer.

"Very well," said Ten. *"I can bring her back, but she will take on a different form. Is that adequate?"*

"Will it still be her?"

"It will."

"And she will be with me forever."

"Yes."

Mason released the breath he forgot he was holding. "Okay. I agree." He lifted his chin to the sky and held out his arms.

The howling wind whipped and danced around him, its invisible fingers brushing against his skin. It carried with it a dark stream, as black as ink, swirling and twisting like a restless serpent. As it wrapped around him, he could feel a shimmer of energy course throughout his body. His sorrow dissipated, replaced with a strange sense of comfort that bloomed within him.

With a sudden and terrifying motion, the dark specter reared up, its foul breath filling the air as it lunged forward, burying its head into his own. His mind was filled with a swirling chaos, threatening to engulf him completely. His forearm burned deep beneath his skin. As he glanced down, he witnessed a symbol slowly appear. Crying out in pain, he watched as the rune appeared like a permanent tattoo.

The whirlwind subsided, the pain in his arm diminished, taking with it his strength. He collapsed to his knees.

CHAPTER 18
FIVE YEARS LATER

A SEETHING mass of star struck youth, their excited chatter filling the air, snaked eagerly around the building. The energy of their wide-eyed anticipation was palpable as they poured into the parking lot, where the scent of pheromones mingled with the stench of teenage body odor. Even more revelers swayed and sung along to the soul-stirring sounds of Ten, his voice resonating in that melancholy way of his.

Les grinned mischievously as he weaved through the bustling crowd, immersing himself in the symphony of vibrant voices and joyful laughter that filled the air. The scent of anticipation wafted around him; a kaleidoscope of sights and sounds. As he observed them, Les couldn't help but savor the electric atmosphere, knowing that soon the fabric of their wretched little lives would be shattered like brittle glass.

Lambs to the slaughter.

The jumbo screen loomed above him, projecting the larger-than-life image of Ten sitting on his majestic throne, his band mates surrounding him, all adorned in intricate body paint and masks.

He grinned wildly, impressed by the sheer grandeur of it all.

Years ago, by human standards, when Ten first came to him with his plan, Les never once questioned whether it could be pulled off; he knew his old friend never failed. However, the sheer scope of this particular accomplishment was so immense that even Les had to stand back in awe.

There was no denying it, Ten was a true master of chaos.

With his mind filled with images of all the carnage and torment yet to come, Les left behind the throng of young people and made his way up to the suite where the band was preparing.

With a grand gesture, he entered the chamber and enthusiastically settled himself onto the plush crimson sofa. After lighting a cigarette, he exhaled a plume of smoke and leaned back against the soft cushions.

Ten stood with an air of authority while his faithful minion delicately applied black and red paint to his body, creating a striking visual design.

"Perfect," she whispered as she stepped back and surveyed her handiwork.

"I must admit Riley," said Les, exhaling another plume of smoke. "The body paint was an excellent addition. You were right, it makes him far more god-like."

She regarded Les with her intense, pitch-black eyes, then shifted her focus back to Ten. With a tilt of her head, she meticulously scanned his body, ensuring she didn't overlook anything. "It's done," she said with that raspy, demonic voice of hers, then she wandered over to a stack of cases in the corner of the room.

Ten took a step back, his eyes fixated on his reflection in the mirror. There was a devious glimmer in his black eyes as a wicked grin spread across his lips.

"My old friend," Les said with a smile as he sauntered across the room and positioned himself behind Ten. "You have outdone yourself. Your sheer mastery and skill leave me in awe, and I bow in tremendous respect."

The demon turned to face him. "I can feel them. Their blind adoration and pure devotion are intoxicating." He moved past Les and made his way to the window where he gazed down at the mass of youthful bodies below. "Tonight is only the beginning."

There was a subtle knock on the door, followed by a sudden burst of energy as it swung open.

"Five minutes," announced the stage manager. Without another word, he turned and made his way down the corridor, his radio squawking the whole time.

The rest of the band entered the room, all wearing disguises of their own design. Les took a moment to look over each one, reveling in the sheer creativity of it all. He flashed a grin and winked at Rain, it was impressive how well she and Nine meshed together. They were a perfect match. "My dear, you are positively beaming with energy this evening," he said.

She winked back at him with iridescent eyes and twirled a drumstick around her fingers.

Riley stood before Ten, her pale gray hands clasping a black and red mask, its intricate design catching the light. Wearing an otherworldly smile, she presented it to him.

He carefully positioned it over his face. After a momentary pause, he spun around and brushed past the others on his way to the stage.

Before leaving the room, Les paused at the threshold and turned to Riley. "Are you joining us?"

Her face broke into a passive grin, stretching from ear to ear. "I'm already with him. There's no need for my physical presence."

Les nodded in understanding, then closed the door with a soft click before heading toward the stage. From this night onward, the world would never be the same.

ACKNOWLEDGMENTS

Welcome to the beginning.

What you just read was the first installment in what will be a four part collection of origin stories for a distinct set of characters.

Once you have had a chance to meet all the members of the band, their real story will begin.

In other words, stick around, I promise you it's gonna be a wild ride.

If you enjoyed this story, please be sure to leave a rating or review.

ALSO BY N.L. MCLAUGHLIN

American Nomads

Lost Boys

Imaginary Dragons

True North

Tricksters

Made in the USA
Columbia, SC
24 November 2024